FLESH OF THE SONS

Cannibal County - Book 2

TONY URBAN
DREW STRICKLAND

PACKANACK
publishing

"And the king said unto her, What aileeth thee? And she answered, This woman said unto me, Give up your son so we may eat him today, and we will eat my son tomorrow.

So we boiled my son and ate him. And I said unto her on the next day, Give up your son so we may eat him, but she hath hidden him."

— 2 KINGS 6:28-29

CHAPTER ONE

IT SEEMED TOO GOOD TO BE TRUE. ONE MOMENT WYATT AND his family had been under siege from the cannibals and the next a cavalry led by the blond-haired Alexander, who both looked and acted like a hero straight out of a comic book, arrived seemingly from nowhere to save them.

As they walked, Wyatt struggled to comprehend this most welcome change of luck. And he wished Trooper was still there to see it. God, he missed that man so much.

Maybe it was the fact that he now had time to think about something aside from being attacked by man-eating bastards. The newfound feeling of safety was a blessing and a curse. And even though Wyatt was surrounded by all these new people, his old friend's absence was even more marked.

Trooper would have doubtlessly been reluctant to accept the help. Wyatt suspected his old friend might have even declined the invitation to their compound to rest and recuperate, or at least made a show of it. He was the strong one. The independent one. The glue. And everything seemed lacking without him.

"What's the matter, brother?" Seth asked.

Wyatt blinked his eyes to clear them of stinging tears. He glanced down at Seth who stared at him from his makeshift seat in the shopping cart.

"Nothing."

"Doesn't look like nothing."

Wyatt examined the others, checking to ensure Seth was the only one who'd seen his weakness. No one else paid him any attention and he breathed a little easier.

"Just thinking about Trooper."

"Oh." Seth let his mouth hang open like he planned to say something more, but either changed his mind or camp up empty handed and closed it again.

Ahead, their mother and Allie conversed with some of the women in the group. That made Wyatt smile. It would be good for Barbara, their mom, to have other women around. Females with whom she could casually converse with in a way that seemed as impossible for Wyatt as speaking Aramaic.

It would be good for Allie too. Wyatt hadn't managed to say a word to her since Pete volunteered to die - sparing Wyatt and sealing his own fate. That asshole had to go and be a hero at the worst possible moment and now Wyatt got to carry around the guilt like a yoke on his neck. He knew that was a shitty and selfish way to look at what went down, but it was true. Just another notch on Wyatt's belt of people he couldn't save.

Supper plodded along beside a middle-aged man who kept tossing a tattered baseball into the desert, which Supper fetched over and over again. Even the dog was happy about their newly expanded group.

So why was he so damned melancholy? Wyatt didn't have time to come up with an answer before one of the men in the group screamed--

"Incoming!"

The path ahead exploded, sending out shrapnel in the form of dirt and rocks. A stone the size of a fist caught a red-haired woman in the forehead, and she collapsed in a spray of blood.

Then, a bullet ripped through the chest of the man who'd been playing with Supper. He dropped to his knees, covering the wound with his hands, but blood forced its way through like water escaping a fissure in a dam.

The dog dashed to Wyatt's side as another round kicked up dust at Alexander's feet.

"Take cover!" Alexander ordered but they were in the midst of a wide-open expanse of Texas borderlands and there was nothing behind which to hide.

Wyatt looked at Seth. "Hold on."

"Why?"

Wyatt didn't respond. Instead he flipped the shopping cart onto its side, wheels facing the direction from which the gunfire had erupted. Seth hit the ground hard and grunted out an *Oof* as Wyatt forced him flat on the ground.

"Supper, stay," Wyatt said.

The dog did as commanded and hunkered in the dirt beside Seth.

Wyatt looked toward his mother, toward Allie. Both were on the ground, hands covering their heads. That was good.

The people who'd saved them, the soldiers or militia or whatever the hell they were, all remained on their feet, trying to source the attackers.

Maybe some danger in his life was what Wyatt needed to shake the sadness that clung to him like cheap cologne. As bullets flew his way, for the first time since being rescued, he was able to forget about Trooper. Forget about what he'd lost. And focus on the new fight at hand.

CHAPTER TWO

BETWEEN THE INCOMING ROUNDS AND THE INITIAL EXPLOSION, the air had turned brown in a dusty fog that made it nearly impossible to see more than a few feet in front of your own face. Through it, Wyatt sought out the soldiers and found them.

The group had locked in on the attackers. They had their AK 47s shouldered and returned fire. After a volley of gunshots Wyatt raced to Alexander's side.

"Where are they?" Wyatt asked.

Even though return fire was hurtling their way, Alexander stood tall. Again, Wyatt was reminded of a comic book hero. Fearless in the face of danger.

Alexander looked to Wyatt, then pointed northwest. It took a moment to make sense of what laid beyond the haze, like trying to see underwater, but soon Wyatt's vision came into focus and he saw them.

Two men, about a hundred yards away, crouched behind a large, rusted out van.

Just as he set his eyes on the pair of men, he saw one of them catch a bullet to the skull. Blood exploded from his noggin, splashing into the van and painting it in brain matter and disintegrated bone.

The other man stared at his dead companion and seemed to lose interest in the gunplay, raising his arms in the air.

"Who are they?" Wyatt asked.

"I'm about to find out," Alexander said. "Care to join me?"

He was walking before Wyatt could answer. Wyatt glanced back at his own group who were still prone on the ground but risked curious looks now that the gunfire had ceased. He knew he should stay with them should anything else go wrong, but he also sensed these new people would scrutinize his every move. It was important to make the right kind of first impression as he was bound to be stuck with it.

He chased after Alexander, breaking into a near jog until he caught up. Alexander glanced at him and smirked. "You've got big balls, Wyatt. I like that."

Ahead, the man left alive came into clearer view. He sported a straggly, gray beard and wore a pair of eyeglasses for which both lenses were cracked. As far as Wyatt could see, he had no weapons of his own, but the dead man's rifle was discarded in the dirt within arm's reach.

"What do you think?" Alexander asked Wyatt as they got closer.

It was only then that Wyatt realized none of the other soldiers had tagged along. "Why'd the others stay back?"

"In case there's more in the party that decided to circle around or flank us. Can never be too careful." He stole a glance at Wyatt. "Besides, if he's got any more bombs with him and plans to go out in a blaze of glory, I'd rather everyone else wasn't blown to bits."

"Oh." Realizing that he'd been deemed expendable didn't make Wyatt feel any better. He had a death grip on his pistol, ready to put it to use at the first sign things were heading south.

"Don't worry, though. I'm sure we're fine."

When they reached the van Alexander went straight to the dead man. He grabbed the rifle off the ground and passed it to Wyatt as he double checked the shooter to confirm his expiration.

Wyatt stared at the man who was still alive. In addition to his unfortunate facial hair his clothing was tattered, and his exposed flesh was covered in a mixture of fresh wounds and healed scars.

"Please," the man said. "He's been holding me captive. Killed my family. Ate my son." He clutched his shoulder with his left hand, covering up a bleeding hole.

"Say that's true. What made you so special that he kept you around? It certainly wasn't your pleasing aroma." Alexander knelt before the man, only a few feet apart. Too close, Wyatt thought. But Alexander also kept the barrel of the AK trained on the man's chest.

"He wanted me alive to torture me. Said my screaming made him laugh." He spat in the general direction of the dead man. It was pea-soup green and thick with snot.

"How'd you two come to know one another?" Alexander asked, his voice flat and impossible to read.

"My family and I was just walking the roads, hoping to find some people or food. Then this feller came along and asked if he could walk with us. He had the gun and we was unarmed so how could we decline?"

"Not the kind of man to take no for an answer, huh?" Alexander stared unblinking at the fellow who seemed to grow more agitated by the word.

"No, sir. That night we made camp and I woke up to my wife screaming. That bastard stabbed her in the belly and split her open like a watermelon. Then he kilt my boy. Shot him dead then toasted him over the fire."

"Roasted, you mean." Alexander's mouth turned up in a slight grin.

"Pardon?" The man's eyes were wide and confused.

"You said he toasted your son over the fire. You toast marshmallows. You roast people. There's a difference."

"I-- I-- If you say so." The man looked past Alexander, toward the others who waited along the road. "Can you folks please help me?"

Wyatt knew it wasn't his place to speak and waited for Alexander to answer. Instead, there came a rifle report.

The man's body slammed into the van as the force of the gunshot hurled him backward. He opened his mouth and groaned, allowing a stream of blood and spittle to spill free, and then his eyes went vacant.

Wyatt turned to Alexander and saw smoke wafting from the barrel of his AK47.

"Why?"

"He was lying," Alexander said.

"How can you be sure?"

Alexander stood. He kicked the newly dead man over. In the small of his back was a rusty revolver and a large hunting knife was sheathed on his belt.

"Not many hostages are armed." Alexander took the man's gun, emptying it of bullets and depositing the lot into his pocket. He passed the knife to Wyatt. "A souvenir. A reminder that there's no room for stupidity in the world anymore. Cannibals, crooks, murderers. They're all out here and you need to figure out who's dangerous and who's not. Otherwise, you'll just be another body in the road."

Wyatt realized how fast Alexander and his group could have mowed all of them down, along with Red and the other cannibals. That they could all be dead in the dirt like these men. "Why'd you trust us?"

Alexander paused to consider it. "You have an honest face."

He broke into a wide smile that revealed near perfect teeth. Of course, Wyatt thought. Just like almost everything else about him.

Alexander gave him a light tap on the shoulder as he stood. Wyatt followed and they headed back to the others. "Papa says there's always room for kindness. And dessert."

Wyatt nodded. He remained grateful this group had found them, and he was even more grateful they judged them worthy of kindness and not a bullet.

CHAPTER THREE

WYATT THOUGHT, AFTER A MORE THAN 2,000-MILE TREK, HE was in good shape. That he could keep pace with just about any man around. But after five hours of following Alexander and his companions, he was dragging. The soldiers seemed as fit as Kenyan marathoners and despite lugging their weapons and gear, they moved at almost twice the usual lackadaisical pace Wyatt had grown accustomed to.

He paused to suck down several swallows of water. He was thirsty but this was more of an excuse for a break. One he hoped wouldn't belie his exhaustion.

"I'll take some of that," his mother said.

Wyatt handed the bottle to Barbara and saw she was tired too. Her hair was slick with sweat and clung to her head like a helmet. The sight made him grin despite his own subpar condition.

"What's so funny?"

"You look like a refugee," he said. "Like we're on the Trail of Tears or something."

Barbara half-smiled but her remaining eye stayed serious. "That didn't end too well, you know."

She was right of course, and Wyatt lost his grin. He hoped their journey had a better ending than that.

It had to. They didn't come all this way just to be locked up or slaughtered. No God could be that cruel. Right?

"Share the love," Seth said. He reached for the bottle which was down to a few sips. Barbara passed it to him. "Thanks. That'll quench my thirst."

"At least you don't have to walk at super soldier speed," Wyatt said.

"Being paralyzed and one-legged does have its benefits." Seth dropped the empty bottle into the cart.

Supper sat at their side and whined.

"Sorry, pooch, I drank the last drop," Seth said to the dog who hung its head in disappointment. "Maybe Wyatt can ask his boyfriend for another."

Seth's mocking smirk annoyed Wyatt but he refused to let it show. Besides, Seth was half-right. Wyatt didn't have a crush on Alexander, but he admired the man's courage and common sense. He supposed, in a way, the man reminded him of Trooper. Maybe that was wishful thinking on his part, but he was eager to find someone to fill that void in his life.

As he stared in Alexander's direction, the man startled him by looking back, almost as if he had felt Wyatt's eyes on him. He caught Wyatt gawking and gave a short wave. "It's up ahead." Alexander pointed to a low embankment. "Just beyond the hill."

Thank God, Wyatt thought as he grabbed the handle of the shopping cart and resumed pushing. If they weren't there soon, he was liable to collapse and that was the last thing he wanted to do with Alexander and the others watching.

Cresting the incline sapped him of whatever strength he had left, but the view was worth it. A hundred yards away, a casino six stories tall jutted up from the desert floor like an adobe monolith. It featured Spanish architecture with half round arches, ornate tile, and wrought iron.

A chain link fence, obviously a new addition since the apocalypse, guarded the property and even at this distance, Wyatt saw people.

"Holy shit," Seth said.

"Seth!" Barbara slapped him lightly on the shoulder.

"What? It's amazing."

Alexander smiled as he hugged his rifle to his chest. He took a deep breath and let it out slowly, nodding his head. "It's not much, but we call it home."

Wyatt realized many of the people behind the fence were armed and appeared to be on patrol. That sight gave him mixed feelings. Staying safe was one thing, but what if this group operated more like a prison than a shelter? What if it was more compound than community?

Before his doubts could take hold, Allie broke his concentration. "I didn't think you could gamble in Texas. Or really, anywhere other than Atlantic City and Las Vegas."

Alexander let out a little laugh. "Once upon a time maybe. But after other states saw the pile of gold they jumped on board. And this place was actually on the Res."

"Res?" Wyatt asked.

"Reservation."

"So, all of you live there? In the casino?" Seth asked.

Alexander nodded. "It wasn't just a casino. It was one of the finest resorts in South Texas. There's plenty of space, lots of suites. And the buffet is amazing."

Seth opened his mouth but stopped when he saw Alexander smile.

"You'll see," Alexander said. "Come on now, enough talking about it. Time to show you our set up." He continued on, scrambling down the hill while the other soldiers followed.

Wyatt stared at the grade. It was uneven and the ground was more chunks of rock and hard caliche than an actual path he could traverse. Sweat slicked his palms as he gripped the shopping cart, knowing it would never make it to the bottom without toppling over.

As if reading his mind, Seth spoke up. "Doesn't look handi-capped friendly. Time to leave me behind and go play with your new friends. I'll just wither away while you guys take some craps."

Wyatt rolled his eyes. "Shut up, dick. And climb on."

Seth wrapped his arms around Wyatt's chest and pulled himself out of the cart and into the piggyback position.

"It's actually shoot some craps, not take some craps." Allie said from their side.

Wyatt looked at her, quizzical.

"What? I grew up less than an hour from A.C."

"I like my version better," Seth said.

Allie nodded toward the shopping cart. "Think we should bring this?"

"Leave it," Seth said. "It can sit up here like a monument to my missing leg."

Wyatt planted his feet in the loose gravel, each step slow and deliberate. The last thing they needed was for him to fall, drop his brother, and have the both of them soar downhill ass over head.

They were a third of their way into the descent when Barbara appeared at his side. "So, what do you think of them?"

"Don't know yet. They're well-guarded and the casino looks secure. And Alexander seems like a solid leader. No bullshit, you know?"

Barb nodded. "I was chatting with some of the women. They seem friendly. Welcoming." She pointed ahead to a tall woman who wore her chestnut hair in double French braids. "That one was a cocktail waitress here. Before."

That surprised Wyatt. He's assumed the lot of them were Army or Marines or maybe some covert special forces. He wasn't expect-ing... normal.

Barbara began to say something else but was interrupted by

Alexander. "I actually used to deal. Most of us knew each other from the casino."

Wyatt was surprised that they'd been overheard, and surprised that their Captain America turned out to be a run of the mill card dealer. Somehow though, knowing these people were just *people*, calmed his unease.

"I would have pegged you for career military," Wyatt said.

"Oh yeah?" Alexander grinned. "What branch?"

Wyatt considered it. "Navy SEAL."

The man coughed out a surprised laugh. "Damn, I'm gonna have to keep you around. You're good for my ego."

Ahead, Alexander's group was almost at the security fence. A middle-aged woman with a ponytail approached from the inside and granted them access.

"And everyone else?" Wyatt asked.

"We've got a few ex-military folks but don't get the wrong idea. We're not survivalists or anything close to that. We just stuck together and gritted it out."

Wyatt watched the man about whom he'd had such a wrong first impression. Knowing that Alexander wasn't all that different from himself, yet seemed to be thriving in this crumbling world, made him feel more comfortable with his own lot in life.

Alexander stopped at the open gate, motioning to the guard. "Friends, this is Fiona. Fiona this is Wyatt, Barbara, Allie, Seth, and..." He flashed another perfect smile. "You promise you're not pranking me? The dog's name is really Supper?"

As he recalled Trooper naming the dog, Wyatt tried not to allow the memory to overwhelm his newfound good cheer. "No lie. That's his name."

"If you say so."

"Welcome." Fiona crouched down and patted her thighs. Supper plodded to her, tail whipping side to side, and licked her face like it was coated in sugar.

Wyatt supposed, if this place was good enough for the dog, it was good enough for him

CHAPTER FOUR

THEY WERE HALFWAY TO THE MAIN ENTRANCE WHEN THE doors burst open and twenty or more people rushed outside. They hurried toward Wyatt and the others, moving in a pack. Aside from the cannibals, he hadn't seen this many people grouped together in years and his hand dropped instinctively to the pistol holstered on his waist.

Before he could do anything stupid Allie slipped tight against him, her body covering his hand, his gun. Hiding his aggressive gesture. "It's okay," she said.

As he looked at the group, he realized she was right. These people weren't a threat. They weren't filthy and unkempt and starving. All appeared well-fed and some even carried a few extra pounds. They wore normal clothes, the kind you'd wear to the mall on a Saturday afternoon.

And they all sported smiling, welcoming faces.

"Sorry for the hullabaloo," Alexander said. "We radioed ahead to let everyone know about you. Like I said, it's been a while since we had new faces. They're an excitable bunch."

As these men and women came to them, Wyatt saw how right he

was. Even though his group hadn't so much as taken a spit shower in weeks, they were greeted with handshakes and hugs. Wyatt imagined this was a small-scale version of how victorious WWII soldiers felt upon their return to the States.

A woman with a constellation of freckles and carrot orange hair emerged from the pack pushing a vacant wheelchair. That was a relief and Wyatt eased Seth into it.

"Shit you people are prepared," Seth said.

Alexander beamed. "We try."

What followed was an almost nonstop festival of welcomes and questions and reassurance that it was safe here. Wyatt had never felt so much raw love all at once, and definitely never from strangers.

"It's like getting off the plane in Hawaii," Barbara said, unable to wipe the smile from her face.

"Except there's no leis," Seth said. Just after he said that, a necklace made from various colors of poker chips was placed around his neck. "Close enough." A smile crept onto his face.

"I didn't realize how much we stank until I was around people who smell good," Allie said as she broke free from a stranger's hug.

"We'll take care of that too," Alexander said. "I can't promise steaming hot water but it's lukewarm and clean." He pointed in the general direction of the gaggle of women. "Ladies, why don't you take Allie and Barbara to get cleaned up?"

The women grabbed onto Barb and Allie's hands and led them away before anyone could protest. Wyatt watched them disappear into the casino. Then he felt Alexander's hand on his shoulder.

"Wyatt, come with me," he said.

He turned to where Seth and Supper had been a moment earlier and saw a few men leading them away.

"Where are they going?" Wyatt asked. He wasn't scared but didn't see the reason for being split up. Some of his initial relaxation faded, replaced with unease.

"Probably to the men's showers," Alexander said. "No offense, but you guys are pretty rank."

Wyatt couldn't see a lie on the man's face, but his body was tense. "Then I should go with them."

Alexander's face showed that he knew what was up. That Wyatt didn't fully trust him. "You can if you want. Everyone here's free to do whatever they choose. But I hoped you'd let me show you around."

Wyatt considered the situation. If Alexander and his people had ulterior motives, they could have killed them at the border, or anywhere and anytime between there and here. He was being overly cautious, maybe even rude, and forced a smile. "Alright."

He followed the man into the casino.

WYATT STOOD HALFWAY BETWEEN THE LOBBY AND GAME ROOM, staring at the garishly colored walls, the patterned carpet that made him almost dizzy. Everything from the handrails to the check-in desk seemed to be coated in faux gold. It was the epitome of 80s kitsch.

A neon sign reading Lucky Eagle hung above the passthrough to the game room. It was at least three feet high and ten feet wide.

"It still lights up if we turn it on," Alexander said, as if reading his mind. "The k burned out a while back, but the rest works."

"You have electricity?" Wyatt asked.

Alexander flashed a grin. "For five hours a day. And we ask everyone to be responsible." He dragged his fingers across the back of a fake-suede couch. "I don't want to get your hopes up too high. We don't have all the comforts of home but we're better off than most. Running water, decent food selection, you name it, we've got your basic needs covered."

Wyatt could hardly believe how fast their fortunes had changed. Less than twelve hours earlier they were struggling through the never-ending abyss of the desert, eating long expired food from cans, boiling water to make it safe to drink, all the while being chased by cannibals. And now... this.

"I don't get it," Wyatt said out loud. "How is everything still so... good, here?"

Alexander opened a door to a side room which led to a long corridor. Fluorescent lights illuminated the passage.

"It's because everyone pitches in. It's not perfect, but it's home."

"Like some hippy commune?" As fast as the words escaped his mouth, Wyatt realized how insulting it must have sounded. "I'm sorry."

Alexander shook his head. "You're not wholly wrong. We work together. We live in relative harmony."

The corridor ended at another door which Alexander opened and stepped through. Wyatt followed and they emerged into a weapons room almost bursting with stock. Some of the other men and women that Wyatt still thought of as soldiers were also inside, returning their AKs to shelves, reloading ammunition belts, changing out of their fatigues and into more traditional clothing.

Alexander pulled the magazine from his rifle and handed it to a man with a bushy, red beard and who reminded Wyatt of a lumberjack. "Want to top that off for me, Ace?"

The man accepted it with a nod and then Alexander began undressing.

"We just take it a day at a time, man." Alexander didn't just have the handsome face of an action hero, but the physique to match. But his muscles weren't the outrageous, trying too hard kind that were earned in a gym. His build was lean and cut. The body of someone who used it, not built it for show. "And most of all, we appreciate all the gifts God has given us and which he continues to send our way. Like you good people."

He stripped down to his boxer briefs then grabbed a pair of jeans and redressed. "So, does that make us hippies?"

Wyatt couldn't hold back a smirk. "Maybe. Well-armed ones, anyway."

Alexander laughed and threw a fake punch his way. Wyatt fake dodged it.

"Don't worry. We won't make you sit around the pool and sing Kumbaya every Sunday."

It was Wyatt's turn to laugh. "Thank God."

"Yeah. That's actually on Thursdays, under the portico," Alexander said.

"Oh, I--"

Alexander ruffled his hair. "I'm just messing with you."

Wyatt was relieved that he hadn't just put his foot in his mouth. And even more relieved that he'd been brought to this place. After everything they'd been through, they deserved some good times.

CHAPTER 5

THE LUKEWARM SHOWER WAS BETTER THAN A DAY AT A THREE-hundred-dollar spa, but that was over now and so was Allie's brief period of relaxation. As soon as she'd toweled off and slipped on a plush, white robe, the mob of women who'd escorted her to the baths were back.

Their kindness was never-ending, from helping her pick out new clothes, to offering her something to eat and drink, to asking her about her past and her time on the road. They were friendly to a fault but having a dozen or more of them surrounding her like a clan of hyenas around a lost gazelle had frayed her nerves almost to the point of snapping.

She felt closed in. Trapped. Her breaths became shallow and quickfire. The women, their friendly faces, blurred into walls of flesh and teeth and clothing that drifted her way and threatened to wash over her like the evening tide. Allie's heart thudded in her chest and her throat tightened. She couldn't even scream. Sweat broke out on her forehead and her vision spun as the world faded away.

Just before she succumbed to the panic attack and passed out, a hand grabbed her arm and pulled her away from the others. There was a voice, firm and masculine, but she couldn't decipher the words. Nonetheless she went with it, brushing against the women in the crowd as the stranger's hand guided her through them.

Whoever had come to her rescue took her away and into a conference room that was wide open and uncluttered. There weren't even any empty folding chairs to take up space. The grip, which had been strong yet caring, released her. She missed the safe, secure feel of that warm hand.

Allie sucked in gaping mouthfuls of air, finally able to breathe again. She'd had panic attacks in the past and she knew the drill. Breathe in and out. In and out. Steady and slow. In and out.

The hand fell onto her shoulder, reassuring, comforting. "Take your time. They mean well, but it can be overwhelming at first."

She was so relieved to be free that she hadn't even thought about who'd rescued her from the crowd. "Thank you. I haven't had a panic attack in years and forgot how--"

"It's okay. You don't need to explain it," the man's voice said.

Even though she was terrified, that floating, drowning feeling would return, she opened her eyes. And the man who stood before her almost took her breath away all over again. He reminded her of a ruggedly handsome actor with his chiseled jaw and intense, sapphire eyes. His salt and pepper hair was a tad on the long side and hung in lazy, unkempt curls across his forehead.

She smiled at him and wondered how the hell someone could make it this far into the apocalypse and still look so damned good. "Well, thank you. For saving me and for understanding my predicament." She gave a light, embarrassed laugh and patted his upper arm, feeling his muscles through his blue chambray shirt.

Oh God, am I really flirting like a schoolgirl right now, she thought and retracted her hand.

He smiled at her, revealing a small gap in his front teeth. It was the sort of flaw that would make an ordinary man look foolish or uneducated, but on him it only added to the charm. "You're welcome. For both. I'm Franklin." He extended his hand to her.

She grabbed it and returned his firm handshake. "Allie."

"Alright Allie, if you're recuperated, would you like me to point you in the direction of some other people your age? They--"

"My age?" She looked him up and down, observing the small wrinkles around his eyes and mouth and tried to judge his. She didn't see how he could be that much older. Five years. Ten tops. "How old do you think I am?"

"No offense intended. I just thought I could introduce you to people with whom you might have more in common."

"So that's that? You storm in there and drag me off without so much as a howdy do and then you try to dump the poor, scaredy cat girl off on other people?" She crossed her arms in front of her. At first, she meant it as a bit of a joke, but the more she considered the way she was being tossed aside, genuine annoyance crept inside.

"If you're insulted then it's my turn to apologize. Maybe I need to start over."

He pushed his hand her way again. She accepted, with less enthusiasm.

"I'm Franklin. And I'm in charge here."

Then it clicked. He was the leader. No wonder he thought he could do whatever he wanted. And there she was on the verge of a toddler's tantrum with the man who ran the place in which they'd decided to seek refuge. Hell of a way to make an impression.

"You're that guy Alexander called Papa?"

Franklin flashed a demure smile and shook his head. "No, I'm not Papa. He's our leader. I just make sure everything stays organized. That everyone's taken care of."

"So, you're like middle management?"

His good cheer wavered, but he recovered fast. "More of the CEO if we're using corporate lingo."

"Second in command then?"

"We're not really structured that way. We don't have commands, or bosses. We're a community and we all have our assignments. Mine is more of a supervisory role, but Papa leads us all. He is our star in the dark sky, if you will."

Allie nodded. She knew exactly what Franklin was saying, but thought his analogies needed a little work. "Alright, I think I get it. Then you're the Little Dipper."

Franklin shook his head at the jab. "Maybe I didn't come off as eloquent as I intended."

"I'll let you off the hook this one time."

"I appreciate that."

She glanced around the empty room, then toward the hall which was equally bereft of people. And with the panic attack fading, the isolation suddenly felt less desirable. "Can you tell me where my friends went? The ones I came in with?"

"They're getting settled in, just as you are. If you follow me, I'll introduce you to some other people. Smaller groups, I promise, so it won't be such an overwhelming situation. Then Papa will speak to us all."

He motioned at the door like a concierge directing a hotel guest toward the sauna and she took that as her cue to leave.

CHAPTER 6

"You're one of the newcomers!"

Barbara sighed before looking to see who'd spoken. She'd enjoyed the privacy of the shower and the break from the people with their never-ending questions, their warm embraces, their wide, prying eyes. She'd hoped it would last longer but no such luck.

After turning toward the sound of the voice she found a small woman who wore her gray hair pulled into a harsh bun. Her face was etched with deep wrinkles and Barb guessed her to be well into her seventh decade.

"Guilty as charged," Barb said.

The woman smiled revealing teeth so perfect they could only be dentures. "As big as this place looks, word travels fast. Everyone's talking about y'all." She grabbed Barbara's forearm and pulled her in close. For someone so tiny and old, she was strong. She planted a dry kiss on Barbara's cheek. "I'm Myrtle."

Barbara shook her arm free. "I'm Barbara." She forced a smile and looked down at her wrist where the imprint of Myrtle's hand lingered.

"Sorry about that. Just got a little excited I guess." Myrtle studied Barbara for a moment. "Not much for strangers, are you?"

Barbara shrugged. "It's not that. It's just that we've been on our own for so long. Years really--"

"Say no more. I have just the thing. Follow me. We'll go around the building to avoid the crowd."

Barbara could tell Myrtle was the type of person who would have greeted new neighbors with a pie or cake upon their arrival. And then insisted on coming into the house and eating it with you, all the while coaxing out your life's story whether you wanted to surrender it or not.

Nonetheless she followed the woman through the back corridors until they came out in a storage room filled with canned and dry goods. It was enough food to last an army a decade or more.

"Wow." Barbara stared at the impressive assortment. While it was reassuring to see the casino was well-stocked, she wasn't exactly sure why Myrtle felt the need to drag her here. "I should probably be going though. One of the other women said there was going to be some kind of announcement."

Myrtle shook her head and moved further into the room. "That'll hold. Nothing moves quick around here. You'll learn that soon enough."

Barbara watched as the old woman pushed aside a few cases of food, then crouched. Her knees crunched audibly but Myrtle didn't flinch in pain. Instead reached deep into a cabinet and fished around with her hand a moment, then broke into a wide grin. "Got it."

What she extracted wasn't a cake or a pie. It was exactly what Barbara needed. A bottle of gin.

"Well shit," Barbara said. "You must be a damned mind reader."

Myrtle unscrewed the lid and passed it to her. Barbara took a large swallow, then paused. She didn't want to look like a pig - or a drunk.

Myrtle nodded. "Drink up. After what you folks have been through, you deserve a nice buzz."

That was the truth, and Barb realized she had earned this. Earned it with her work. Earned it with her suffering. Earned it with her loss. She closed her eyes and took another long swallow and began to cry.

"I can't even imagine what you've been through," Myrtle said. "Thank Papa that Alexander found you when he did, right."

Barb wiped her cheeks with her free hand. That turn of phrase struck her wrong. Whatever happened to Thank God? "Thank *Papa?*"

"Oh," Myrtle laughed, giving Barbara a slap on the arm. "Not like that, honey. Thank Papa as in, thank him for having the foresight to assemble the protectors."

Barbara handed the bottle back to the woman. "Thank you. I did need that." She was still unsure about the Papa talk, but the warmth of the booze made it easier to tolerate.

"As I suspected." Myrtle took a sip and replaced the lid, then returned the bottle to the cabinet.

"You back there, Myrtle?" A man's voice called from the other end of the kitchen.

"You already know I am, or you wouldn't be asking." Myrtle winked at Barb. "You can't break wind in this place without everyone knowing."

Footsteps sounded against the concrete floor as the man approached. "Cassie told me she saw you heading in there with our new friend."

Myrtle rolled her eyes. "Told you."

Barbara hadn't seen a soul on their trip here and wondered how that was even possible, but didn't have much time to consider it before the man came into view. She blinked twice, trying to clear her eye, because at first glance he looked so much like her dead husband that she thought it was him.

"Are you okay, miss?" He asked. His voice carried a strong British accent.

She closed her eye again. Longer, composing herself. When she opened it, she realized the resemblance had been a trick of her mind, at least for the most part. The build was similar, and this man had the same kind eyes and dark brown hair that was graying at the temples, but the similarities ended there. "Sorry. I'm fine."

He raised an eyebrow at Myrtle. "You get her pissed already?"

Myrtle laughed. "I'm an old woman. Don't drink anything stronger than ginger ale and even that's only when my tummy's upset."

He shook his head, but grinned. "You're incorrigible." He looked to Barbara. "Don't let Myrtle corrupt you. She's one of the bad seeds around her."

Barb couldn't hold back a smile. "Is she now?"

"The worst." He extended his palm to her. "I'm Richard. I'm one of the good ones." His grip was strong, but gentle and his skin had the rough texture of a man who'd spent many years working with his hands.

"Barbara."

"Pleasure to meet you."

"Same here." Suddenly she remembered her scarred face. Her horrible, disfiguring injury. He turned her bad side away from him instinctively.

"You mind if I steal her away from you Myrt?"

"Not at all." Myrtle pointed a finger at Barbara. "Any time you need to clear your head, you find me, honey."

"I will."

She followed Richard out of the kitchen and into a hallway decorated with bright, striped wallpaper and a myriad of posters featuring supposedly famous guests of the casino, but the only one Barbara recognized was Blake something or other from *The Voice*.

"I apologize for that," Richard said.

"For what?"

"For letting Myrtle get her claws into you. She has issues with personal space." He held his hand up, curling his fingers like talons.

She stared at him, his joke going past her. "Right," she muttered.

"Well, so much for my humor," he said.

She finally caught on and shook her head. "No, it's... Yeah, funny. Her claws." She mimicked him except she added a *Rawr* sound and immediately hated herself for it. "Sorry."

"Don't be," Richard said. "I rather like you, Barbara. You've got pluck. Now how about you allow me to give you the five pence tour."

Barbara couldn't hold back a smile. "I'd like that. Thank you."

CHAPTER 7

As soon as Seth was out of the shower and redressed, Supper leapt in his lap. Even though he considered the mutt Wyatt's dog, he thought of them as something of kindred spirits. Two creatures who had each lost a limb and were outliers amongst their peers. He hoped Supper felt the same way.

As he wheeled the both of them out of the room and into the hallway, he realized the crowd that had been so eager to greet them was nowhere to be seen. His family too was absent. A hell of a way to make him feel welcome and part of the supposed community.

"Well this is kind of fucked up. What do you think, Supper?"

He wasn't sure why being excluded shocked him. It was the story of his life. Most people didn't mean any harm and he tried not to take it personally. They simply didn't know how to act around a paralyzed person. It was like throwing them into a room with something exotic and unusual. Like a platypus.

After losing use of his legs, he's grown accustomed to being left out. He didn't get invited to birthday parties because there were steps to his friends' houses. Roller and ice skating get-togethers were also nonstarters. Even the rare occasions he was invited to join his buddies at the movies were awkward because he had to sit alone up front and get a crick in his neck from staring up at the screen while they sat in the cushy seats at a normal distance.

In some ways, the apocalypse was good for him because, as everything else turned to shit, his handicap became less concerning. And when his friends all moved away and it was just his family and Trooper, he stopped feeling left out. But now, around all these new people, it was like the first day of school all over again. They got to know each other and explore while he sat alone and isolated.

Shit, what a pity party I'm throwing for myself, Seth thought. He hadn't allowed himself to wallow in a while and just as he was working up a good case of righteous anger ceiling mounted speakers crackled to life.

"In five minutes, Papa will address everyone in the courtyard. Please find yourself a spot. Good luck and good love."

He heard footsteps and shuffling as people moved, he presumed, to the courtyard. A few men and women passed him by, not bothering with a 'hi' or 'howdy' or 'hey there cripple can I give ya a push?' The most he got was a nod, but the majority of them pretended they were blind to anything from their neck down and didn't see him at all.

The hall had emptied by the time Seth worked up the gumption to turn his chair and begin wheeling himself in the direction the others had gone. He made it a few yards when a door to one of the rooms opened and a steady, electric whine spilled out.

Supper's ears perked up at the foreign sound and Seth stopped. A moment later, one of the heftiest people he'd ever seen in real life emerged. The man rode a motorized scooter that crept along only at a pace only marginally quicker than the average tortoise. When he was in the hallway, he turned to close his door and saw Seth watching him.

"Well hello there." His voice had a heavy southern accent and he shared a genuine smile that lit up his face, which was as big around as a basketball.

"Hey." Seth wheeled himself closer. It was nice to be acknowledged, even if the guy who finally greeted him was a real-life version of Jabba the Hutt and looked to be pushing sixty-years-old.

His white hair was pulled back in a loose ponytail and he wore an equally crisp, white guayabera shirt and linen pants. An angry, purple scar covered much of the left side of the man's face and neck and, from what Seth could see, it looked as if it might extend down his gargantuan body.

"There's a meeting or speech or something in the courtyard," Seth said.

"I heard. Do you know your way?"

"Not really."

"I can show you. Shall we roll there together?"

"Sure."

They continued down the hall, making a right, then another right.

"Your dog's quite handsome. May I pet him?"

Seth nodded and the man tentatively reached toward Supper who watched with mild interest and allowed his head to be scratched.

"I see the both of you share a malady."

Seth glanced at his stump and nodded. He then looked to the man and saw he wasn't watching the dog, but him. His scar was more obvious up close and appeared to be some sort of burn. Intermixed with the thickened, rough skin were boils or sores. Odd growths that looked like acne from hell. It was tempting to stare but Seth made a special effort not to, as he'd spent the better part of his life on the receiving end of such gawking.

Still, the man's unabashed inspection made him both uncomfortable and annoyed. "So," Seth said. "Are you paralyzed too?"

The man gave a low, breathless chuckle. "Not paralyzed. Just fat."

Seth wondered how it was possible to stay so fat in a world where food - real food - was in such short supply but saw little reason to be rude to the first person who'd treated him like, well, a person.

Ahead, light spilled through a series of sliding glass doors which were open, allowing a chorus of chatter to spill inside. Seth wasn't eager to join the masses, to again be different, and slowed, allowing the man to pass him by.

The man also hesitated. He half-turned his scooter toward Seth so he could look him in the eye. His gaze was so earnest and prying that Seth thought he might be reading his mind. Then he opened his mouth and seemed to confirm that.

"I've been different the better part of my entire life," the man said. "And I used to loathe the attributes that made me stand out in a crowd. The perceived faults that made others look down upon me. But there came an incident, maybe I'll share it with you some time, when I became enlightened. I became aware that what made me different also made me unrepeatable. A markedly unique person unlike anyone else. And I embraced my differences. You should too, my child."

A striking, middle-aged man stepped through the open doors and drew the attention of both the fat man and Seth. "Everyone's waiting, Papa."

Seth wanted to shake his head to make sure he'd heard what he thought he heard. That this corpulent, scarred man in the scooter wasn't just another rando, but Papa himself. The man everyone here spoke about as if he was a Greek God crossed with the King of England.

"I'm aware, Franklin." Papa never looked away from Seth as he spoke. "However, my attention at the moment is on this fine, young man who has brightened our community with his very presence. Tell me, child, what is your name?"

Seth opened his mouth to speak but it was so dry his tongue stuck to the roof of his mouth. He conjured enough spit to loosen it, then croaked out, "Seth."

"A pleasure, Seth. And I mean that sincerely. Won't you please join us in the courtyard?"

Although he still struggled to believe any of this real, Seth nodded.

"Franklin, be a dear and guide my new friend outside and ensure he has a place up front."

Seth thought Franklin looked annoyed, or at least peeved, at being ordered, but the man didn't protest out loud. He stepped behind Seth's chairs and took the handlebars. As he pushed, Seth noticed Supper eyeing Franklin all the way, the fur on his scruff raised to attention. He put his hand on the dog's back to calm him. The last thing he needed was Supper going all Tasmanian devil and attacking.

Seth was first out the doors and embarrassed to find nearly one hundred people staring in his direction. Crammed into the small area the crowd appeared even larger and more impressive. And they all looked at him. He wondered if this was how rock stars felt when they walked on stage. He was mostly uncomfortable with the attention, but as his heartbeat quickened, he realized it was somewhat intoxicating too.

And then everyone burst into cheers. He almost raised his hand in a wave when he realized their eyes were no longer on him. They were looking beyond him.

To Papa.

CHAPTER 8

THERE WERE SO MANY PEOPLE IN THE CROWD - A HUNDRED OR more - that Wyatt thought he had little to no chance of spotting his mother, Seth, or Allie. He stood on his tiptoes, trying to find their faces in the throng of strangers, but had no luck.

"They're in there somewhere," Alexander said.

"I know. I just--" Before Wyatt could continue, the speakers rang out again. This time, instead of an announcement, there was music. It was an instrumental piece featuring trumpets and a piano. It sounded somewhat familiar, but certainly wasn't the kind of tune you could dance to. It was the style of music they played to announce the arrival of a President. Or King.

And then came the cheering and applause.

Wyatt was staring upward, thinking that the man who garnered such a reception must be high above them, like the Pope on Easter Sunday. His eyes drifted across the balconies but saw no one. That's when Alexander put his hand on his shoulder.

"Not up there. Papa's down here. With us. Because he's one of us."

He pointed at ground level and Wyatt followed his finger to a set of nondescript glass doors which opened to a random hallway. Through them came an obese man on a motorized scooter. Not any different from the people Wyatt would need to sidestep in the grocery stores back home.

This is their hero, Wyatt thought.

Papa raised a hand in a wide, arcing wave as he rode the scooter toward a microphone that waited on a stand. Franklin, a tall, middle-aged man, walked at his side but unlike Papa his face was sober, his eyes alert. If he'd have been wearing a black suit Wyatt would have pegged him for Secret Service and he wondered if he was some sort of bodyguard.

Not that it seemed as if Papa had anything to fear from this crowd. Movie stars received less impressive ovations. He even saw a few women, and one man, crying tears of joy over Papa's arrival.

He looked to his side and found Alexander beaming, his face in a kind of rapturous awe. How did this ordinary man garner such fanfare? Wyatt struggled to understand it.

Upon reaching the microphone stand, Franklin began to lower it so it would be at face level, but Papa shook his head and said words which were inaudible over the din of the crowd. Then the man, with great effort and a fair amount of sweat, managed to push himself to his feet. Franklin held his elbow, steadying him.

With that, the crowd fell silent. The only noise that remained was a soft breeze and Papa's wheezing into the microphone.

"Greetings, my children."

The crowd spoke almost in unison. "Hello, Papa!"

"Have you heard the good news?" He paused a theatrical beat. "We're having fresh peaches with dinner this evening."

The people roared with laughter. Wyatt didn't see the humor but smiled so as not to stand out in a bad way.

"Of course, there's other good news. Truly good news. Miraculous, really. We've welcomed five new friends into our community today."

Papa's eyes scanned the crowd but, unlike Wyatt, he had no

trouble finding who he was looking for and gestured with a meaty paw. "Barbara Morrill came here all the way from Maine."

Wyatt watched everyone turn to his mother who stood on the left side of the audience. Even at a distance he thought he saw her blush at the attention as she gave a brief wave.

"Her boys are here too and from what I've been told they're bona fide heroes. They are Wyatt."

He pointed and Wyatt felt the pressure of more than one hundred sets of eyes on him. It was like standing in front of the largest classroom he'd ever seen, only these people weren't class-mates. They were strangers. He wanted to tuck his head and melt into the floor, but Alexander squeezed his shoulder.

"Relax. Enjoy your moment," Alexander said.

Wyatt nodded to the crowd but was eager for the attention to turn elsewhere. Fortunately, it did.

"And Seth," Papa said.

Wyatt found Seth sitting by the doors from which Papa had emerged, the dog in his lap.

"And we mustn't forget their loyal dog who was given the unfor-tunate name of Supper. But don't you get any ideas now."

Seth lifted Supper's paw and made the dog wave to the crowd. Papa guffawed and the crowd roared. Even Wyatt couldn't hold back a chuckle, but some of that might have been relief that the people were now examining someone other than him.

"Last, but most certainly not least, is the lovely Allie Hagan," Papa said.

Wyatt joined in with the gawking crowd and found Allie standing on the sidelines. He hadn't seen her cleaned up in weeks and he gulped in a quick breath when he saw her. Maybe it was being in this environment rather than on the road or in the desert, but she looked more beautiful than ever, even though he could see her smile was both nervous and fake.

The crowd's incessant clapping and whooping continued until

Papa tapped the microphone with his hand, sending back a shrill protest of feedback

"Alright, alright. I know you're all excited, as am I, but please remember that our new friends have been on their own for quite some time and respect that they shall require time to acclimate. Please, let us not overwhelm them."

Silence again reigned.

"Their story is one of perseverance. Survival. A want - no, a need - for something more. Having no idea if a better place was out there but taking a leap of faith. Well, I say it is no coincidence that they have shown up here, to our home, to our *community*. Some might say it was a stroke of luck that they happened upon us from so far away. But I say NO!" The word boomed through the speakers and made Wyatt flinch.

"There's no such thing as luck, my children. These people, like all of you, were guided here by the strong hand, the loving hand, of Yahweh. And for that, we must all say, 'thank you'!"

Papa bowed his head and the crowd did the same. Wyatt heard a chorus of muttered prayers of thanks. After a few moments everyone returned their attention to the big man.

"Now, I'm aware that I might sound like a kook," Papa said.

"No way!" Someone shouted from the crowd.

"It's alright. I know, I know. Especially to the newcomers, I'm sure our ways might come off as eccentric. Perhaps, even weird."

He chuckled and the crowd laughed. But he was right. Wyatt did think this was all a little weird.

"And that's okay. If you'd have told me, ten years ago, that I would have survived nuclear attacks and that I would help build a safe haven for all who need Yahweh's protection, I wouldn't have believed it either. But He showed me the way. He led me out of the burning ashes and the stinking brimstone of Hell on Earth. He saved not only my life but my soul. He took this broken man that would have once laughed at the idea of a place like this and turned me into His humble servant. He showed me the light and the way."

Many in the crowd said, "Amen" and everyone raised their hands into the air in praise. Wyatt again felt like the outlier for not joining in, but also felt doing so would be wrong somehow because this was all too new and foreign to him and mimicking their actions solely to fit in seemed offensive.

He looked to the people he knew, to see how they reacted. Allie's arms were folded across her chest. Barbara's hands were in her pockets. But Seth's were upraised. Wyatt tried to examine his brother, to find the signature smirk pulling his mouth up and to the left, but it wasn't there.

"Now is the time to stand up for what is important to us. What is important in life. Nobody can take what is ours. Not anymore. We stand strong. We stand together. All of us knowing we are the chosen people to carry on. And we welcome those that join us and smite down those that mean us harm.

"And again, we say Amen!"

The crowd repeated, "Amen!" together.

Wyatt watched as Papa turned around and walked the few steps to his scooter. He didn't accept help from Franklin, he did it all on his own. Then he rode off from where he came.

When the man was side by side with Seth, Papa leaned in close and seemed to whisper something in his ear. Wyatt watched his brother smile and nod.

"Looks like your brother is special," Alexander said.

Wyatt peeled his eyes from Papa and Seth. "Why?"

"He's getting a one on one."

Wyatt turned back and saw Franklin pushing Seth, following Papa. "Is that strange or something?"

"I wouldn't say strange," Alexander said. "But Papa's got his hands full keeping this ship afloat. Doesn't leave him a lot of time to socialize."

"So, why'd he pick Seth?"

Alexander shrugged his shoulders, then glanced skyward. "Every decision he makes comes straight from the big guy above."

Wyatt wondered if all these people believed Papa had a direct line to God. And whether Alexander was fully on board or towing the company line. The look on his face made Wyatt think he was a true believer. Or one hell of an actor. Either way, it wasn't a conversation he wanted to continue at the moment.

"Is it okay if I go talk to my mom and Allie?" He asked.

"Of course," Alexander said. "This is your home for as long as you choose to stay. You're free to do anything you want here, Wyatt. All of you are."

He waded into the crowd. Wyatt realized Alexander wasn't the only person smiling, they all wore faces that appeared downright exuberant. It was a welcome change of pace from the grim reality of life on the road, but he couldn't shake the lingering feeling that it was all too perfect.

CHAPTER 9

FRANKLIN UNLOCKED THE DOOR TO THE SUITE AND HELD IT AJAR as Papa passed through. Seth hesitated, looking up at the man whose face wore a smile that didn't quite reach his eyes.

"Should I--"

"Go on," Franklin said. "I'm not holding open the door to air out the room."

Seth wheeled himself into the suite, immediately struck by its size. He thought the biggest rooms in hotels were reserved for the upper floors, but this was the largest he'd ever seen in person. Crisp, white carpet and furniture gave it an airy, almost Heavenly feel and he checked the floor behind him to ensure his wheels weren't dirty and leaving marks.

The entryway opened to a kitchenette which in turn led to a sprawling living room area, complete with white, plush couches and chairs. A bar stood against the far wall, which also contained two doors leading to the bathroom and bedroom. The door to the latter hung half-open and through the gap Seth saw a lingerie-clad woman asleep on the bed. He had a good view of her heart-shaped bottom but tried not to gawk.

"I'll be out in a moment, my child," Papa's voice seeped through the same doorway. "Make ya'self comfortable." His voice lacked some of the heft it had carried outside, now sounding more genial. His deep southern accent came out harder too.

Seth wondered how comfortable he was expected to be, alone in this lavish room. Was he supposed to sit on the couch? Make a sandwich? Pour himself a drink? A little specificity would have been nice.

Without it though, he decided to play it safe and wait in his chair. That was easier anyway as Supper was busy napping on his lap.

When Papa emerged, he'd changed into a new white shirt, but this one was unbuttoned and sagged open, revealing his ample chest and gut. Both were criss crossed by purple veins and stretch marks. Wiry gray hairs poked up from his flesh like bristles. The man used a cotton towel to wipe sweat from his neck, then under his pits.

Seth found this a little like seeing the Wizard hiding behind the curtain. Gone was the mystique of the man who'd rallied his people into a gleeful frenzy. In his place was an ordinary fat man with perspiration problems.

Papa's willingness to allow Seth to see him in such a state could have tarnished him in the boy's eyes, but it had the opposite effect. Instead, Seth was more in awe because he knew he was seeing parts, both physical and emotional, of the man to which others were not privy. He knew he was receiving special treatment and for a young man who'd so often been excluded, this reversal of fortune was intoxicating.

"I tell you something I've learned the hard way," Papa said. "A man doesn't understand the glory of air conditioning until it's been snatched away from him."

Seth smiled politely, as one does when they're in a stranger's home for the first time and have no idea what to say.

Papa limped to the couch and plopped down, the springs screaming under his girth. He stared at Seth. "You ever been to Texas before?"

"No, sir."

"I appreciate the respect, child, but you can drop the sir."

"So just *Papa* then?"

"I know, I know. Kind of eccentric, right? It's just a nickname that stuck, I suppose. One I was reborn with in this new world." Papa grabbed a glass of bourbon off the marble coffee table and took a sip. "Oh, my. Now where are my manners? Would you like a drink?"

"No. I'm fine. You don't have to get up."

"Nonsense, you're my guest." He leaned forward with a grandfatherly smile that put Seth at ease. He half-expected Papa to reach behind his ear and pull out a quarter. "Anyway, I'll just have one of the wives to fetch it." He slapped Seth's knee and chortled a blend of a cough and laughter. Phlegm roughing up in the back of his throat with each chuckle.

"Wives?" Seth said. "Like, plural?"

Papa winked. "Belle, why don't you come on in here and fix our guest a drink, m'kay?"

"No, really, I'm--"

A stunning woman with ice blonde hair emerged from the bedroom. She wore a silver, paper-thin nightgown and Seth didn't have to look too hard to realize that was all she was wearing. Her nipples poked against the fabric like daggers. Again, he fought the desire to stare.

Seth stammered as she walked by, sending him a small smile on her way to the bar. The first words he managed were, "That's not the same one I saw on the bed."

Papa chuckled again. "No, I don't suppose she is, now, is she?" He leaned in again. "You know, her name is Belle, short for Jezebel. I swear to Yahweh. I thought she was a stripper givin' me her stage name first time we met, but no, that's the name her momma and daddy gave her. Prescient folks, they were."

Belle returned from the bar, glass in hand. She bent down as she passed Seth the drink, at the same time providing him with a complete and perfect view down her gown. His mouth went dry as sawdust and now he was glad for the drink.

"Th-- Th-- Thank you."

"Many thanks, beautiful Belle. Now why don't you go on back to the bedroom and relax with Destiny?" He patted Jezebel on the butt as she passed by him and left the room. Then, Papa turned to Seth. "Destiny. Now that *is* a stripper name."

"A stripper? One of your wives?" Seth gulped down a good third of the liquid in his glass, an act that sent him coughing and wishing for water to put out the fire that consumed him from the inside out. "Jesus Christ," he gasped.

He'd never been a boy to ration his swearing but as soon as the words spilled from his lips, he realized his mistake. He's just taken the Lord's name in vain in front of a preacher - of sorts, anyway. He half-expected the man to throw him out of the room. To kick Seth and his family out of this community before they even had a chance to settle in. And it would be deserved.

Instead, Papa only pointed a pudgy finger at him. "Easy on that sort of talk around here, my child. You can say fuck and shit and piss all you desire. Throw in some cocks and cunts if you must. For those are only words. But I won't tolerate blasphemy."

Seth nodded, cowed. "Understood. I'm sorry."

"Apologies to me are not necessary or required. But I reckon you might want to repent in your prayers tonight."

Seth took another drink and cringed.

Papa's stern expression transitioned to a smile. "That's some of the smoothest bourbon you can find anywhere these days."

Seth set the glass down and wiped the water from his eyes. "Thank you. Very smooth." He shivered. Supper glanced up at him, annoyed by all the fuss. He patted the dog's head. Everything's cool, friend. I'm just getting drunk with Papa.

"I know you're young but I'm curious about something. Do you think there's a reason, a purpose, for what happened five years ago?"

That's a pretty heavy question, Seth thought. As he tried to come up with an answer Papa continued.

"I believe Yahweh decided to reset the world, giving everyone a chance to start over. Be it a stripper, nun, charlatan, pastor, or even a cripple." He narrowed his eyes down to Seth. "I imagine you might know something about that, now, wouldn't you? Heck, I know a thing or two about that, as well."

Seth noticed a thin, viscous fluid seeping from one of large sores that held residence on the side of Papa's face. As if reading his mind, the old man pulled out a white rag from his pocket and dabbed at one of them, leaving small specks of blood on the cloth.

"You and I are very alike. I can tell. And it's not only the physical side of the coin of which I speak. It's the mental." Papa leaned in close and tapped Seth's forehead, and then did the same to his own. "I was a hunk of raw clay, worthless and useless, but Yahweh himself molded into me the man I am today. I was made to do great things. And I'm telling you now Seth, so are you."

Seth listened to the man in front of him. He watched him speak. Something about it seemed so genuine. It was as if Papa peered into his mind, saw what he wanted out of life, and was now telling him it was within his reach. And this wasn't a superfluous, pandering, *miracles can happen* kind of speech. It was the knowledge that, if he believed in himself, he could have everything he ever needed.

"I know, to a young soul such as yourself, the hour is early but it's nearing time for me to retire." Papa opened his mouth in an exaggerated yawn.

Seth was disappointed. He wanted to hear more of Papa's message, receive more of his wisdom, but he knew better than to be rude. He nodded and backed his chair away from the table. "Of course."

"Our people are good people. Introduce yourself, socialize. But I hope you'll also take time to reflect upon what we've discussed."

"I will. I promise."

"That's good, my child. Very good. You head on out now."

Leaving Papa was the last thing Seth wanted to do, but he wheeled himself to the door, all the while wondering what this really meant. Would Papa have this same conversation with Wyatt? With their mother and Allie? Being dismissed so soon made him wonder if this spiel was the standard greeting and he'd just been played a fool.

Seth opened the door to the suite and found Franklin standing outside. He was so surprised by the man's presence that he flinched. Franklin noticed and grinned. Prick, Seth thought.

"Franklin," Papa called out and the man peered into the room.

"Yes, Papa?"

"Would you be a dear and take Seth to his room?"

"I don't think they've been assigned rooms yet," Franklin said.

"Maybe not the others. But I want Seth in my hall. I believe one oh nine is vacant."

Seth saw Franklin's eyes narrow but didn't know why. This didn't feel like the time to ask either.

"Anything else?"

"Make sure he has a good meal this evening. Double portions. He's had a hard journey."

Franklin nodded. "Will do." He went to close the door, but Papa's voice stopped him.

"And Seth, do join me for breakfast tomorrow. I so look forward to continuing our discussion."

Seth watched Papa hobble to the bedroom. "You'll forgive me, but the ladies can't be kept waiting." He stepped inside and closed the door. Then Franklin shut the door to the suite, rattling its frame. Seth noticed the number on Papa's suite was 113.

"You need a push or?"

Seth shook his head. "I'm good. Just tell me which way to go."

Franklin pointed to the right and strode that way. Seth followed, passing 111 and stopping at the next room. His room. The man swiped a plastic keycard and the lock opened. Franklin handed him the card and pushed open the door, gesturing with his hand like Vanna White after a contestant decided to buy a vowel.

"All yours, kid."

Seth peered into the room. It wasn't quite as large as Papa's but was still three times as large as any hotel room in which he'd ever resided.

"I'll get you some grub, but I need to piss first." Franklin turned back up the hall.

"You can use my bathroom," Seth said, trying to curry favor.

Franklin flashed a joyless smile. "That's fine. I'm right next door." He moved to room 111.

"Aren't you like second in command," Seth asked.

Franklin nodded as he opened the door to his own suite. "So they say."

"Then what does that make me?" Seth was unable to hide his cocksure grin.

Franklin stopped bothering with the fake cheer. "New. It makes you new. And be aware, this place is like a Ferris wheel. You might start out on top because you're fresh and have a good sob story, but most don't stay there long." He disappeared into his room.

Seth wondered if there was any truth to his words, but decided they sounded more like the tartest of sour grapes. Papa knew he had potential. Papa knew he was special. And soon, so would everyone else.

CHAPTER 10

The loudspeaker woke Wyatt with a hard crack that sat him bolt upright in bed. His hands clawed at the sheets, searching for a gun, a weapon, anything he could use to fight and protect his family when--

"Breakfast will be served in the dining hall in thirty minutes."

That was going to take some getting used to.

He rolled onto his side, rubbing his eyes as he shook off the deepest, most peaceful night's sleep he'd enjoyed since leaving Maine. He was surprised to see what passed for daylight spilling through the room's floor to ceiling windows as he hadn't slept past the sunrise in months.

He climbed out of bed and walked to the window, taking in the view that mostly consisted of solar panels - what appeared to be acres of them. He was surprised they got enough light to power this place, even if it was for only a few hours a day, but supposed it was a quantity over quality deal. Beyond them stood hundreds of windmills which spun lazily.

"Pretty cool," he said to himself.

As he turned away from the window and toward the chair upon

which he'd thrown yesterday's clothing, his eyes went to the bed. He considered climbing back in. After seasons on the road where he slept in the dirt or on hard floors, the bed was like a siren's song, beckoning him back into its gentle, caressing embrace.

Only now the sight of the empty bed made him frown because it reminded him that he was alone. He thought about his mother and Seth. And Allie. Where had they all spent the night? He appreciated that they'd all been given their own room, but why separate them? The unease he'd felt the previous evening returned with a vengeance.

He slipped on his pants and was half into his shirt when loud pounding shook the room's door. Wyatt went to it hoping to find one of his people. Instead, he was met by Alexander.

"Hey Wyatt. You ready for some grub?" He was decked out in his usual desert camouflage uniform.

"Uh, yeah. I guess." He finished pulling on his shirt.

Alexander shook his head. "Get out of those clothes. Take these." Alexander handed him a fresh set, everything from socks up. "We'll drop your other stuff at the laundry. You're not out in the wild anymore. You don't have to wear the same clothes two days in a row."

"The laundry?" Wyatt asked. This place really did have everything.

"You'll get used to it sooner or later, but I'm telling you, your life's changed for the better. And after what you've been through you earned it."

Wyatt appreciated the idea, but he found it difficult to think that he would ever get used to it. He paused, waiting for Alexander to step out of the room so he could change but the man lingered. Instead of undressing and redressing in front of him, Wyatt slipped into the bathroom.

"What's on the menu, anyway?" Wyatt asked.

"It's a casino, man. What do you think? Breakfast buffet all the way."

"No shit?"

"Don't get your hopes up too high. The eggs are powdered and so's the milk for the cereal. But it's edible and I imagine a damn sight better than the crap you've been surviving on."

He was right about that. And Wyatt thought again that it was going to take a long time to accept such luxuries.

Wyatt recognized many familiar faces on the way to the dining hall but couldn't remember many names, so he kept his head down and only nodded and mumbled "Hi" when he accidentally made eye contact. Social skills were going to take a while to return.

Alexander led him past the slot machines and tables like they were rats funneling through a maze. From there, signs pointed the way. They were left over from the days before and still proclaimed offers like "All you can eat!" and "Free drinks!" He doubted that was true now, but he wasn't going to complain.

He smelled the food a good hundred yards before they even reached the dining hall and he hadn't realized how hungry he was until the aroma slapped him in the face. Without realizing it, an audible sigh escaped him. "Mmm."

Alexander glanced back at him, grinning. "I told you."

The hall was filled with residents seated at tables, enjoying their breakfast at a leisurely pace. Even that seemed foreign to Wyatt, who'd grown accustomed to wolfing down his food so he could get on with life. This reminded him of the cafeteria in his old school, albeit much fancier. It reminded him of how life used to be.

Wyatt and Alexander grabbed trays and got in line. He knew there'd be eggs and cereal, but he was disappointed to see that was almost the extent of it. The only other option was fruit cocktail which had the all too familiar signs of coming from a can.

"I might have oversold it," Alexander said.

Wyatt glanced back at him. "No, I mean, it's just—"

"We're running a little low at the moment, but I promise you we'll have more variety soon. But hey, at least in the meantime our bellies will be full."

"Absolutely. I can't imagine anyone complaining about free food."

"You've obviously never had kids," Alexander said. The corner of his lip turned to a small smile, but his eyes quickly went soft, as if he was reliving a memory that he'd hidden away deep inside. This was the first Alexander had mentioned anything relating to a family, but Wyatt knew better than to push the subject when it seemed as if it didn't have a good ending.

As the men filled their plates, Wyatt scanned the cafeteria for his family and Allie. It was hard pinpointing anyone in the sea of faces, but he eventually found Barbara sitting at a table with a few strangers.

"You wanna come back and eat in the security room?" Alexander asked.

Wyatt felt bad about abandoning his new friend, but he wanted to reconnect with the others, to see how their first night had gone, and because he missed them.

"If you don't mind, I'd like to catch up with my mom. And Seth and Allie."

He thought Alexander looked disappointed, but the man put on a smile. "Absolutely. It's good that you have family here."

That made Wyatt feel even more like an ass, especially on the heels of Alexander's remark about children. "Why don't you join us?"

Alexander shook his head and waved him off. "You go ahead and enjoy your time. I've got some assignments to work on."

"Like paperwork?"

"It's not all firefights and rescue parties. Most of my job's planning and logistics. Boring crap." Alexander flashed him a wink, making Wyatt feel a little better about ditching him. "If you stick around long enough, you'll get a job too, so enjoy yourself now."

They turned away from each other and Wyatt moved to his

mother's table. Three women sat with her and Wyatt could see in her expression that she was annoyed but trying to hide it.

"Morning, mom."

Barbara looked up with relieved, almost desperate eyes. "Wyatt!" She jumped up from her seat and gave him a quick, but firm, embrace.

It felt good to have her arms around him, but they had an audience and he gently shook himself free. "Did you eat yet?"

She motioned to an empty tray which sat before her. "I did. Why don't you take your tray and we'll catch up outside?"

He knew she was searching for an out, a break from the people, and he didn't blame her. "Sounds good."

"Aren't you even going to introduce us?" An older woman at the table asked.

Barbara's face scrunched with mild annoyance and Wyatt tried to fight off a laugh as she turned back to them. "Wyatt, this is Myrtle. And that's Meagan and Sunny."

"Nice to meet you all."

They smiled and parroted the same.

"That mother of yours is a firecracker," Myrtle said.

"She sure is," Wyatt said. Barbara squeezed his free hand. He knew the drill. "If you ladies will excuse us."

As they slipped away Barbara whispered, "They were two minutes away from inviting me into their sewing circle. I can feel it."

"Look at you, making friends."

Barb rolled her eyes. "They're nice. Don't get me wrong. But it's too much too soon."

As they passed through the room, then into the halls leading to the courtyard, Wyatt understood what she meant. Everyone who saw them stared a little too long with too much interest. He wondered if it would be days or weeks until their appeal wore off.

As if the big guy upstairs had heard his thoughts, the courtyard was void of others. They moved to a bench and sat side by side.

"Where'd you spent the night?" Barbara asked.

"They gave me a room on the fourth floor. You?"

"Second. I think the room assignments are based on age. The younger you are, the more stairs you get to climb."

"You might be right." He shoveled a bite of eggs into his mouth. They were lukewarm at best and had a faded, stale taste but it had been so long since he'd consumed real, fresh eggs that it was hard to remember exactly what they were supposed to taste like.

"Have you seen Seth?" He asked.

Barbara shook her head. "Not since he went off with Papa after the big welcome announcement."

"What was up with that anyway?"

"Your guess is as good as mine."

"Franklin said he's interning or something," Allie said.

Wyatt and Barbara turned toward the voice and found Allie approaching them with a tray of food. Wyatt didn't realize how much he'd been missing her until he saw her face. She'd put on makeup that made her eyes look like they belonged to a model and her cherry red lipstick was downright kissable.

He jumped up from her seat and nodded to the new vacancy. "Here you go."

"I could have stood." But she took the seat anyway.

"What were you saying about Seth?" Barbara asked. "What do you mean *intern?*

Allie took a sip of the cereal milk. "Don't know. But I guess the big dude likes him. He's staying in the same wing as Papa and Franklin."

That was the second time she'd said that name and Wyatt liked it less every time it came out of her mouth. "Who's Franklin?"

"From what I gather, he's sort of the little boss, if Papa's the big boss anyway. But Franklin said Papa really likes him."

Wyatt looked to his mother and raised an eyebrow. "I never knew him to be the type to make good first impressions."

Barbara grinned. "I guess he found the right ass to kiss."

That made Wyatt laugh so hard it almost hurt.

"You're doing pretty good too," Allie said to him. "You and that Alex guy seem awful chummy."

"He showed me around. Told me a bit about how everything works."

"Is that all?" Allie winked.

Wyatt didn't enjoy being on the receiving end of her teasing, even if it was playful. Maybe his mother realized that and jumped in to change the conversation.

"What are your thoughts on Papa anyway? Aside from the name which, I hope we can all agree, is terrible."

"He was different than what I was expecting," Allie said. "But not bad. Just... different."

"Well, I think we'd all agree on that," Barbara said. "But I was more interested in your thoughts on his message."

Wyatt had been thinking about that most of the prior night but hadn't made up his mind just yet. "He knows how to work a crowd."

"I thought his speech was really inspiring. What he said, it made me feel like I could be a part of something here. Something good for a change," Allie said.

"You should hear what the other women say about him," Barbara said, her voice dropping a little lower even though they were alone. "Apparently, he sleeps around like a Kennedy."

That image gave Wyatt a whole-body shiver and he fought to block the mental imagery from his mind. "Oh, no. Let's not go there."

Allie giggled. "You're such a prude, Wyatt." She gave his thigh a playful swat. "Besides, he probably deserves all the ass he can get. He brought this place together. And look around, everyone here's so happy. And there's food. And they're safe. Franklin said--"

She went on but Wyatt's ears were ringing with that man's name. He'd heard enough. "Who gives a shit what Franklin says?"

"I do, for one."

Everyone snapped toward the man's voice. Franklin stood several yards away, his defined arms folded across his chest. Wyatt thought he looked like a middle-aged male model. The kind that did commercials for hair color or laxatives.

"Wyatt, Barbara, this is Franklin," Allie said.

"I gathered." Wyatt gave a brief wave. Franklin nodded and strode their way. Two other men who each wore black windbreakers and jeans lingered behind him and didn't follow. They waited behind like mafia goons who only jumped when Simon said jump.

"Morning everyone. Allie, I hope your quarters were satisfactory." Before she could answer, he addressed all of them. "I don't mean to interrupt your breakfast, but if you all would come with me, it would be greatly appreciated."

"Look, if this is about what I said, I didn't mean anything--"

Franklin flashed a wide, reassuring smile. "No, I promise you it's nothing to do with that. And it's nothing bad at all." He patted Wyatt's shoulder in a fatherly way. A way Wyatt didn't appreciate it. "Feel free to bring your food," Franklin said.

Before Wyatt could protest, they were being escorted out of the courtyard by Franklin and the two guards.

CHAPTER 11

As his group passed through the cafeteria, Wyatt stole furtive glances at the people dining. He tried to read their faces, to see if anyone was sending out red alert vibes to clue him in that danger awaited.

If there was a reason to be concerned, none of them let on. Most were more interested in their food, but Wyatt nonetheless felt the hair on the nape of his neck standing at attention. Nothing about this felt right.

While Wyatt, Barbara, and Allie followed Franklin, the guards kept pace at the rear. The lot of them continued through the casino and up a narrow hall before coming to a stop in an empty conference room. It was only then, when no other people were around, that Franklin spoke up.

"I apologize for the inconvenience, and I suppose, the theatrics. We just didn't want to make a scene in front of the rest of the community."

"You didn't want to make a scene? So, you and the Braindead Bruiser twins lead us away like we're being taken to the gallows?"

"Wyatt!" Allie slapped his arm.

That made Franklin grin. "I suppose it could have been handled a little better."

"Who the hell are these guys anyway? And where's Alexander? I want to talk to him about this bullshit." Wyatt looked the two large guards up and down. Even through their clothes it was evident they were roped in muscle. So much that Wyatt wondered if they'd stumbled upon a stash of steroids and were putting them to good use.

"I can clear everything up, *if* you'll let me finish, Wyatt," Franklin said, irritated at the series of interruptions.

Wyatt looked to the women who remained tight lipped. He wondered if either of them shared his worry or if they thought he was overreacting. Probably the latter as the looks they gave him were telling him to shut his mouth. Maybe it was better to let the man finish.

"First of all, it was never our intent to scare you, or make you feel as if we had sinister intentions. I thought after yesterday that was apparent. And to answer your questions, or demand, I should say. Alexander is the protector for our community. He handles anything that involves our security outside and in. But this isn't a security issue."

Wyatt nodded and allowed his shoulders to slouch. Ever since Trooper's death he'd been on a constant state of alert. Determined that no one else he loved would die on his watch. It was exhausting, both mentally and physically and the muscles in his neck felt like they were tied in knots. He tried to relax as much as he could while Franklin finished his spiel.

The man waved his hand toward the two guards. "These two gentleman, the Blockhead Bruiser twins, was it?"

Wyatt shuffled back and forth on his feet and looked to the ground, lifting an eyebrow. "Braindead Bruiser twins, actually," he mumbled. He looked up at the two men who held their position, but stared with blank, robotic faces.

"Ah, yes. The Braindead Bruiser twins. Very clever. Ron and

William are Papa's personal security. He wanted to make sure that you understood this message was from him."

"Wouldn't it have been easier for him to come out and tell us all this himself?" Allie asked.

"As I'm sure you noticed, he has mobility issues. Besides, if he'd have come to the cafeteria in person... Well, let's just say that would cause much more of a scene than what we just did."

"So, what's this message?" Wyatt asked.

Franklin's gaze lingered on Allie a little longer that Wyatt liked. "It's simple. We heard that you've been asking questions about being here. About your station here. And he wanted to make it clear that you are free to go any time you'd like. You are our guests. We welcome you to stay, but know that if you'd like to leave, just alert us to your desire."

"We have to ask permission?" Wyatt asked.

Franklin nodded. "I appreciate the paranoia, Wyatt. It's probably what got you from Maine all the way down here to Texas. It's a good thing, especially in a world like this. But you'll find that it is an unnecessary tool within these walls. The reason we need to know your plans is so we can see you off safely with supplies and with the cache of weapons you had when Alexander and the others rescued you."

Wyatt thought he stressed the word rescue. As in, you owe us. But that might have been his bruised ego.

"The gates are guarded and can't be opened without orders from myself or Alexander. Or Papa, of course. That is for all of our protection as I'm sure you'll come to understand."

"That sounds fair," Allie said, nudging Wyatt in the side. "Wouldn't you say so, Wyatt?"

There was something about Franklin that Wyatt didn't like. He'd been captivated by Papa yesterday, and he had befriended Alexander, but Franklin was a different animal. He knew it wouldn't be reasonable to expect to like everyone in the community, but this man left a sour taste in his mouth.

"Why were we split up yesterday?" Wyatt asked, unable to keep his mouth closed and go with the flow.

Franklin gave a hollow laugh. "Wyatt, you are something else. I promise you, there was nothing sinister about it."

Allie kept needling him in the side and Wyatt finally met her gaze. Her mouth didn't move but the message was clear. Shut up.

"Alexander radioed ahead to let everyone know they were on their way and gave us a report about who you were. There was a lot of excitement and everyone wanted to make you feel welcome. We're a friendly bunch but I'll admit it didn't occur to us that you'd likely be more comfortable staying together as you got your bearings. I apologize on everyone's behalf, but we only wanted to show you all that our community has to offer."

Wyatt nodded, satisfied even if part of him thought this all seemed too rehearsed. "Alright. And I think I speak for all of us when I say that we appreciate being allowed to stay here. And also, grateful that we can leave whenever we'd like."

"We never hold anyone against their will, here. There's no need," Franklin said with another of his charming smiles. Allie nudged Wyatt even harder.

Wyatt knew exactly what the woman wanted of him and he gritted his teeth. "And I suppose I got ahead of myself when I became accusatory. I didn't mean to come at you so hot."

"No offense taken," Franklin said. "The community is your family, and vice versa. At least, if you let them."

The conversation seemed to have reached its conclusion, but to put a final pin in the discussion Alexander stepped into the room. He gave Wyatt a quick but distracted nod as he moved to Franklin. He spoke low and Wyatt strained to hear. "I'd appreciate an audience," he said. "We need to get another trade going asap."

Annoyance clouded Franklin's face. Wyatt wasn't sure whether it was Alexander's demand or the fact that it had been made in front of the new arrivals. Either way he put on a phony smile and turned his attention from Alexander to the others.

"If you'll excuse us." He nodded to the two guards who opened the door for Wyatt's group to leave.

Rather than cause any more of a scene, Wyatt moved with his mother and Allie toward the door. Until Alexander's voice stopped him.

"Not you, Wyatt. I want you in on this."

CHAPTER 12

WYATT WATCHED WITH A SORT OF CONFUSED AWE AS PAPA hobbled out of the bedroom, leaning on a cane that looked destined to snap under his heft. The man looked even bigger up close and personal. It wasn't only his actual size either. There was something akin to an aura around him, a presence. Wyatt thought he'd feel the same sort of gravitas if he were sharing a room with a President or King. Then he realized, in a way, that's what he was doing.

He stole a glance at Seth who watched Papa with rapturous attention. He'd been surprised to find his little brother in the room when he arrived with Alexander and Franklin. Surprised and happy.

Seth seemed pleased to see him too but, for a moment, Wyatt thought he looked disappointed as well. Like a kid who'd just realized that the bag of candy he'd been given was now meant to be shared. Wyatt tried to tell himself he was reading too much into a split-second expression, but the thought nagged at him even more now that he realized Seth was riding shotgun on the Papa bandwagon.

The big man shuffled past a glass coffee table and half-sat, half-collapsed onto the couch. He burped out an *Oof* that almost made Wyatt smile, but he knew that would not be an appropriate or welcome reaction, so he kept it inside and distracted himself by scratching Supper under his chin.

Alexander had been standing by the window and took a step closer. "Papa we need to get out there and--"

Papa held up his hand. "Alexander, please. I know you take your position here very seriously and for that I am grateful. Truly I am. But I haven't even greeted my new friend here and whatever you need to say will surely hold for another half minute, will it not?"

Alexander pinched his lips together and gave a brief, silent, nod.

"Thank you." Papa turned toward Wyatt, giving him a too good look at the sores on his face and neck. They reminded Wyatt of a sunburn he'd got one time at Gooch's Beach. Wyatt had peeled through three layers of skin on his back and shoulders, but whatever had burned Papa was a thousand times worse.

"Nice of you to join us, Wyatt," Papa said. "Some spirits to wet your whistle?"

Wyatt shook his head. "Thank you, but I'm fine."

"As you wish. However, if you reconsider please speak up. If you need a testament to the quality of my bourbon, ask your brother. I'm sure he'll recommend it highly."

Wyatt saw Seth smirk and his cheeks blaze pink. He was surprised at how chummy the two had become.

Papa grabbed a glass of booze from the coffee table and sipped it as he leaned back into the couch, its plush whiteness swallowing him up. "Alright. Now that pleasantries have taken place, Alexander, tell us what's got you so fired up at this early hour."

"We need to head out and make a trade. We're running low on vitals."

"A trade mission? With whom this time?" Papa asked.

"The hermit would be our best bet. We have a few pallets of electronics we scavenged last month and those always pique his interest."

"I see. And what is it we need? Specifically?"

"Food, sir," Alexander replied.

"Drop the sir bullshit, Alexander. You know the drill."

"Sorry, Papa."

Papa waved his hand, dismissing the comment. "I can always get behind more food." He looked at Seth, grinned and winked. "And our efforts at growing haven't exactly yielded bountiful results thus far."

Franklin cracked the knuckles in his fingers, one at a time. The noise drew Papa's attention and, Wyatt realized, that was the intent.

"You'll give yourself arthritis, Franklin. It would be easier and less painful to simply speak when you have something to say."

Franklin's expression was blank, but Wyatt thought he saw fire behind the man's eyes. "I think it's a mistake."

"Explain," Papa said.

"The squad just got back yesterday after almost a week on the outside. They're drained. They need time to recuperate."

Papa looked from him to Alexander for a retort and Alexander obliged.

"We'll be fine. My people are tough."

"No one's doubting that," Papa said. "You and your people are heroes to every last one of us. That's why we want you to be safe. Now, are you certain this isn't too soon? Surely we have enough supplies to last a fortnight or more."

"Dried and canned goods, yes. But people have become accustomed to fresh fruits and vegetables too. And that'll be exhausted within a few days."

Papa exhaled with enough force to send phlegm rattling in his throat. He washed it down with another mouthful of alcohol. "Alright, then. I trust your judgement and for you to get back here in one piece."

"Of course. And I'd like to take Wyatt with me," Alexander said.

Papa looked to Wyatt with kind, curious eyes. "And what do you want to do, Wyatt?"

"I'm down."

The man chuckled. "You're *down*. Such bravado. How old are you?"

"Eighteen."

Papa gave a wistful smile. "My oh my. If I was your age and had myself that pretty little piece you came in here with, I doubt you'd be able to pry me out of her with dynamite." He leaned forward, elbows against his knees. It was a posture that amplified his gut and reminded Wyatt of Buddha. "Tell me. Why are you so eager to go back out into the weeds rather than shacking up in one of our luxurious rooms with Miss Allie and doing your best impression of rabbits in heat?"

It wasn't a bad question. One Wyatt hadn't considered. And now that it was presented to him, he realized just how stupid he was being. He'd spent months out there, every second his life in danger. Now he'd found safety and less than 24 hours later he was ready to abandon it. What the hell was wrong with him?

At the same time, he knew he wanted - no, needed - to prove himself capable. To Alexander. To Franklin. To Papa. Maybe even to himself. Because his first go around in the wild had left men dead and even though he couldn't bring them back, he had to make penance.

But he couldn't say all of that. "I want to contribute."

Papa nodded. "Very noble of you. Well, I don't need to tell you about the risks. And Alexander here says you handle yourself well."

"He does," Alexander said.

"You're a man, Wyatt. If you want to go, and Alexander wants you to go, then I'll leave it at that. His team, his decision."

Wyatt was relieved and nervous. He was about to ask Papa for some of that booze when Seth broke the silence.

"Take me with you."

Alexander opened his mouth to speak but Papa cut him off before he got a word out. "No, Seth. You aren't going. Your condition would be a detriment to the others."

"Just because I can't walk doesn't mean I can't handle myself. I killed more men out there than Wyatt!"

"I'm unsure that's information worthy of a brag," Papa said.

Whatever cockiness Seth had conjured vanished. "I didn't mean it like that. I just--"

"I'm not saying you are incapable of fighting. But you must take others, and their safety, into consideration."

Seth crossed his arm, petulant. "I didn't know I needed permission to leave."

Papa's smile slipped from his face, and for the first time, Wyatt thought he sensed fear, or something close to it, from the other men as he saw them exchange glances.

"You don't. Y'all can leave if you want to. Nobody's gonna stop you from doin' that. Go, now. I'll have Franklin radio the guards at the fence."

Seth couldn't meet Papa's gaze and looked to Wyatt with wounded, puppy dog eyes. Wyatt knew his brother wanted him to come to his defense, but he was certain doing so would seal all their fate.

"It's your decision, brother," Wyatt said.

Papa reached out and rested his hand atop Seth's knee. "If you want to be a part of this community, and I truly hope you do, you need to take my advice. Got it?"

Seth swallowed hard, nodding. "I don't want to leave. I just want to help."

In a flash the big man's expression returned to warm and loving. "And I welcome your help. Here. With me."

CHAPTER 13

WYATT HELD HIS BREATH AS HE STOOD BEFORE THE CLOSED hotel room door, hand raised to knock but hesitating. It would be easier to walk away and avoid the drama, he knew that as sure as he knew his own name. But he was also aware that, should he tuck tail, he'd always wonder *what if*.

So, he knocked.

"Room service," he said.

Maybe she's not in there. Maybe she's hanging out with some of the other women. Or Franklin. That latter thought made him feel sick.

He heard bed springs squeak from inside the room, then soft footsteps.

"I didn't order anything," Allie said. "I didn't even know they had room service."

The lock flicked audibly, then the door pulled inward. Allie stood behind it, peeking out. In one hand she clutched a hairbrush while the other still held the doorknob. Her hair was a wet, frizzy mess, one half of her head still in dreadlocks. The other unfurled and hung in kinky strands.

"Wyatt?" Allie stared, confused or surprised or both. She stepped out from behind the door revealing that she was wearing a white cotton bathrobe.

"What happened to your hair?" He tried to hide the shock, both in his voice and on his face.

She flashed a nervous smile. "I figured, since I was back in civilization it was time to brush out my dreads. Didn't realize quite how much work it would be though. My arms are cramping so bad I can hardly lift them."

She turned away from him and headed toward the bed where a menagerie of hair products was spread out. "Come in and make yourself useful."

He watched her sit on the edge of the bed and grab a spray bottle which she used to saturate one of her dreadlocks.

"What are you waiting for?"

He wasn't sure. The sight of her on the bed, in her robe, made him uncomfortable. He remembered that day at the lake when he'd seen her completely nude in the water. How they came together. How they were on the verge of so much more until--

He pushed the memory to the side. Because as sweet as that encounter with Allie was, it was followed by Trooper's vicious, horrible end. And that was the last thing he wanted to remember.

Wyatt closed the door behind him as he entered the room, then moved to her. She pushed the brush in his direction, and he accepted it, confused. "What am I supposed to do?"

"What do you usually do with a hairbrush? Just be gentle."

She lifted the wet dread to show him where to use it and he worked the bristles into her hair, using about as much care as he'd have used if tasked with handling a piece of fine, antique china. There was resistance, but he went slow and eventually the strands of hair began to come loose and separate.

"How'd your big meeting go?" She asked.

Her voice was teasing but he thought there was some gravity behind the words.

"It was fine," he said, dragging the brush through her blonde tresses.

"Are they going to kick us out?"

"What? No." He looked her in the eyes to make certain she believed him. "We're good here."

"I hope so. Because this is the first time, I've felt safe in years. Since... it all ended. I forgot how good that felt. And I don't want to lose that."

"I don't either."

"It didn't seem that way this morning. You and Franklin were like two roosters putting on a show for the hens."

That stung because it was true. Wyatt hadn't realized it had been so obvious. "Sorry."

"You should be." Some of the seriousness left her face. She even worked up a smirk. "So, are you going to tell me what the meeting was about, or did you make some sort of blood oath of secrecy?"

"It's nothing secretive. I'm going with Alexander's team to make a trade for food."

Her smirk vanished. "When?"

"Tomorrow."

She sighed. "I don't know why you're so fucking eager to get yourself killed."

He ignored that for a while until he heard her sniffle and saw a tear spill down her cheek. Wyatt withdrew the brush and sat it on the bed. "I'm not going to get killed."

Allie stared down at the bed until he took her chin and turned his face to him.

"Why are you so worried?" He asked.

"Why aren't you?"

It was a fair question but, before he could think of a good answer, she continued.

"I'm tired of letting myself love people only to lose them."

Wyatt wasn't sure he heard her right. Even if he had, she didn't mean *love* the way he wanted it to mean. If she loved him it was the way she'd love an annoying, little brother.

Right?

He had to know. "You mean you--"

Allie took his hands in hers. "I need you, Wyatt. Here. With me." She pulled him closer to her, close enough to kiss. And that's what she did. Her lips felt like velvet against his own and he wanted to get lost in the moment, but all he could do was wonder why he hadn't brushed his teeth after breakfast and how bad his breath was.

She didn't seem to mind though, pushing her tongue into his mouth, massaging his. Allie grabbed a fistful of his hair, drawing their bodies even closer together. He felt her heat through the robe and slipped his hand between the soft cotton folds where it found her breast and caressed. She gave a soft groan which made him hard as steel.

They fell onto the bed, hands desperate, yearning. He felt her unzip his jeans, push them over his hips. He untied the loose knot that held her robe shut.

Their bodies pressed together. Connected.

As she drew him inside her he felt on the verge of losing his mind. Her breaths came fast and humid against his face. And she whispered into his ear.

"Promise you'll come back to me," she said.

Their bodies rocked, rhythmic, smooth, in sync.

"I do."

Allie rolled on top of him. Her lithe figure rising and falling. Rising and falling. "Promise me you'll never let anything bad happen."

If his head had been clear he might have hedged on that one, but in the moment he was helpless.

"I promise."

CHAPTER 14

WYATT WATCHED THE GATES OPEN BEFORE HIM. HE STOOD WITH the group of seven men and two women, waiting to venture out of the community to bring back food for everyone.

Alexander had set him up with a desert camo uniform, so he fit in with everyone else, but Wyatt noticed that, while close, the uniforms didn't quite match. Some had patches and badges. Faded areas where name tags had been removed. Rust-colored stains that could only be blood.

The clothes were used and abused, but he supposed, from a distance, they got the message across. This was a unified team. One with which you didn't want to fuck. That had been his first impression of them, when they saved him and his family from Red's band of cannibals.

Alexander had also set him up with an AK47 of his own and even though he'd never fired such an impressive and intimidating weapon before, he supposed he could manage. Besides, Alexander had promised him there'd be no trouble and that carrying the weaponry was akin to tossing a spare tire into your trunk. The odds you'd ever need it were slim, but it was good to have, just in case. For further back up, he'd been supplied with a pistol and two full magazines.

As the gate came open and he stared into the unending desert ahead, he realized it felt good to hold the rifle against his body. It made him feel secure that he could handle anything that might come their way.

Alexander nudged him. "You ready for this?"

It surprised Wyatt to realize he wasn't sure. Even after just a few days inside he'd reacclimated to a life where he didn't have to listen for every branch snap or footfall. Where he didn't have to keep alert to what was at his sides and behind him. Where he didn't need to live in a state of constant fear. It felt like a whole lifetime ago that they were on the road, trying to find a better life for themselves. Was he ready to go back out there?

"I guess we'll find out," Wyatt said with a grin.

They walked and no one said much. That part was familiar and the silence of life on the road came back to him like a tidal wave. Soon he was back in the pattern of putting one foot in front of the other and not thinking about when, or if, the journey would end.

"Want a bite?" a man said.

His voice startled Wyatt who'd been sitting apart from the group and gulping water to hydrate his parched mouth and throat. They'd been on the road for five hours, maybe six, and broke for lunch. Only Wyatt hadn't thought ahead and packed anything for himself.

While the group seemed to accept him into their party, he hadn't felt comfortable enough with them to beg some food. It wasn't like he'd spent much longer periods of time hungry, after all.

When he glanced at the man who'd spoken, he saw a face covered in stubble and his own reflection in mirrored sunglasses. Then he saw the man's hand was extended and in it he held a candy bar. He looked to be in his thirties with a round face and his right cheek bulged with enough tobacco to give the impression that he was smuggling a golf ball inside his mouth.

Wyatt half-smiled. Something inside him was always ready for pushback, yet here this man was, offering him a bite of his Snickers. He really needed to stop worrying so much.

"Nah, I'm good. But thanks," he glanced at the nameplate on the man's uniform. "Weston."

The man shrugged and shoved the remainder of the candy bar into his mouth. "Name's actually Clark," he said through a mouthful of nougat. "Uni came with the name and I'm too lazy to cut it off. Anyway, fuck it, I don't got a nickname so go with Weston if it's easier to remember." He folded the candy wrapped into a triangle and flicked it Wyatt's way, then snorted out something akin to a chuckle when it ricocheted off his cheek.

Wyatt watched the man and thought he seemed a little off. Socially awkward, or maybe even on the autism scale. But who was he to judge?

"Don't stand too close to Clark. He thinks it's amusing to mark his new friends by pissing on their boots," Alexander said.

Wyatt glanced his way and laughed. But when Clark only shrugged Wyatt stopped laughing. "You're serious?" he asked Alexander.

"Sure am."

Clark flipped Alexander the bird. "You're just jealous because I didn't water your flowers, pussy."

Alexander extended his hand to Wyatt who took it and let himself be pulled to his feet, suddenly eager to put some distance between himself and Clark. "I'm real glad you took the initiative to come with us. Some people are meant to be kept behind the walls. They'd never make it more than a day out here." They walked west, ahead of the others. "Not guys like you and me though. I can already tell you're one of us."

"I'm glad you asked me. Don't get me wrong, life at the casino's pretty damned terrific. But I don't want to get a free ride either. I'm willing to do whatever I can to help."

"That means a lot to me. To all of us." Alexander turned back to the others. "Break's over. Get to stepping."

They rose and followed. It felt odd to be in the lead again, but Wyatt knew he really wasn't. This was Alexander's show and he was along for the ride. Nothing more, nothing less.

"How far away is this place? Where we're going to trade, I mean." Wyatt asked.

"It's another eight or so miles. We could get there and back in a day but there's no sense running ourselves into the ground," Alexander said. "We can camp there and head back in the--"

Woosh.

Wyatt felt a cool wind blast past his cheek. It happened so fast he didn't realize what was going on until he heard one of Alexander's men scream. His head snapped toward the miserable cries and saw a four feet long spear embedded in the man's chest.

The man fell to his knees, but the spear kept him propped upright. His hands clawed at the weapon, desperate as blood turned his tan camo red and ran down the weapon, pudding in the dirt.

The guy, with whom Wyatt hadn't even exchanged a simple 'Hello,' went limp less than five seconds later. Probably not even enough time to comprehend what was happening to him. Wyatt could barely understand it himself.

It was the second spear that hammered it in.

A man further back in the group caught it in his throat. It jutted from his neck, two feet of wood on either side. The man tried to speak, or scream, but all that came out was a mouthful of blood and incomprehensible gurgles as he collapsed to the ground.

Wyatt's hands fumbled for the AK that was slung over his shoulder but, before he could get a grip on it, he saw another man impaled through his face and the sight made him remember a time his parents had taken him and Seth to a fancy restaurant where he skewed grapes with plastic swords.

"Where the fuck are they coming from?" Clark screamed.

Wyatt saw him spinning around, rifle ready to go off at any second and he finally got a grip on his own weapon. His hands were slick with sweat as he clutched it, unsure where to aim.

"There," Alexander yelled. "Get into formation, they don't have guns. Take them out."

Wyatt saw Alexander pointing at an embankment to their left and he could make out a small group of men using a dilapidated shack for cover. Meanwhile, Wyatt's group was exposed with nowhere to hide. To prove that point another spear flew through the group, missing Clark by inches.

"Motherfuckers!" Clark shouted.

The gunfire erupted. Wyatt watched two of the assailants fall. One careened off the building and rolled down the hill.

More spears flew their way, but none of them landed their target. As his group returned fire Wyatt remained frozen, thinking about that first spear and how close it had come to impaling him.

He stood, frozen, with his heartbeat sounding like claps of thunder in his ears. He realized he wasn't breathing, that he was shaking all over, and that he couldn't make his body do anything but stand there and be a sitting duck.

Before he could die on his feet like a fool, Alexander grabbed hold of his shirt and forced him onto his knees. Wyatt realized everyone else was on the ground and shooting but he still couldn't clear the fog in his head and make himself join in the fray.

Then Alexander bellowed into his ear. Wyatt wasn't sure if it was to make himself heard over the gunfire or because he was pissed off. Either way, the message was the same. "Get your head on straight and shoot those fuckers!"

That harsh check was exactly what Wyatt needed. He raised his rifle, aimed, fired. The first bullet went wide but the second found its mark. It punched through the man's cheek which exploded in a spray of blood and bone as he collapsed.

The other soldiers rained hell on the attackers who screamed and bled as they died. Wyatt found a young man aiming a spear, seconds from throwing it, and sent two rounds into his abdomen. His eyes grew wide and shocked and Wyatt realized he was still a boy. Younger than himself, maybe by five years. He tried not to think about that as the fight dwindled and soon all the attackers were dead.

Wyatt's ears were ringing from the gunfire but through it he heard Clark's big mouth. "Those cocksuckers killed Pat and Benny," Clark said, spitting to the side as he looked at his dead buddies.

"And Ramon," one of the women said, staring at the guy who'd had the bad luck of getting impaled through the face,

"Everyone else okay?" Alexander asked.

Wyatt looked to them as they nodded, affirmative. He couldn't believe how fast it had all gone down, and that it was really over. It was yet another reminder how horrible life was out here, and he wished he'd have stayed at the casino after all.

"Wyatt, Clark, Laurie, come with me and let's make sure we got 'em all," Alexander said.

Wyatt walked with them to the bodies. Clark trekked up the hill. Alexander kept a watch on the road ahead and behind while the others began to kick at the bodies piled up at the base of the hill.

"All clear up here," Clark said.

"Good, let's get--"

"Holy fuck, this one is still alive," Laurie, a middle-aged woman who wore her black and gray hair in a loose ponytail, said.

Wyatt and Alexander jogged to her. She stood over the boy Wyatt had shot. One of the bullets had shattered his collar bone. He clutched at the right side of his chest with his hand, blood oozing between his fingers. Alexander kicked the boy's arm and his hand fell away, revealing a gunshot wound just north of his nipple.

"Who shot this one?" Alexander asked.

"I did," Wyatt said.

Alexander turned to him and Wyatt thought he saw something like pity in his eyes. He realized Alexander wasn't the super soldier he'd envisioned him to be. That he hated death as much as any normal man. That made Wyatt feel relieved, to know that he wasn't the only one who felt this way, until--

"Then finish him off," Alexander said.

Wyatt shifted his gaze from Alexander to the boy who stared up at him with pained, bloodshot eyes. "What?"

"These fuckers killed our own. They were going to eat us, the sick fucks," Clark said.

Wyatt glanced around the group. He wasn't going to find any backers here unless he came up with a damned good reason.

Or maybe he should just kill him and be done with it. He let the barrel of the rifle drift toward the boy's face and saw his eyes grow wide with fear and panic. Wyatt's finger caressed the trigger.

Just do it, he thought. Clark's right. They're cannibals. This kid would have killed him without a second thought if they switched places.

But they were supposed to be better than the cannibals. What was the point in surviving if it meant you had to become a savage? This boy was unarmed and no threat. This wasn't shooting someone in the heat of battle or self-defense. This would be murder. Surely the others had to see that too.

"We need to take him back," Wyatt said. "You can question him. You and Papa. Find out if there are more. Where they're living. If they know about the casino. Information is every bit as important as food."

That sounded so good. Wyatt almost believed it himself and he was sure it was going to work.

"Fucking pansy ass pussy," Wyatt heard one of the men mutter.

He was losing hope, but he knew the only opinion that mattered was Alexander's. He looked to him, pleading.

Alexander turned away, but not before Wyatt saw a look of disgust in his eyes. "Get the wagon and load him up."

"Whatever you say, boss," Laurie said.

Alexander grabbed Wyatt's arm and dragged him away from the

others. His grip was a vise and Wyatt couldn't believe how strong, and how furious, the man he already thought of as a friend, was.

When they were out of earshot Alexander shifted his grip from Wyatt's arm to his chin, his nails digging into the soft flesh under his jaw. "Don't you ever undermine my authority again. Out here, I am Papa, you got it? He chose me to be the protector and that means I make the decisions."

He pushed Wyatt away, collecting himself and some of the anger either faded, or he made an effort at concealing it.

"Do you understand?"

Wyatt nodded. There were no words to say. Alexander had made it very clear already.

CHAPTER 15

PETULANCE CAME EASY TO SETH. ALWAYS HAD. ENDING UP IN the chair only made it easier to fall into the frame of mind that the world was against him and that pouting was the best option.

His pity party for one was taking place in the parking lot at the rear of the casino. He stared at the windmills and solar panels and played the earlier meeting on repeat inside his head and with each recantation he only became more pissed off.

What else did he have to do to prove himself? He'd fought off cannibals. He's survived gunfights. He's killed men with his teeth. When were these assholes going to understand that he was as good as the rest of them? Maybe even better.

Wyatt hadn't come to his defense. That annoyed him, but he wasn't surprised. His big brother had a habit of treating him like a China doll, something delicate and easily broken. Seth supposed that went with the territory of being the elder sibling. But it was Papa who had denied him the chance to go out there and show the men what he could do.

That hurt.

Because Papa had pretended to understand him. The man had

blown up his ego like a hot air balloon and Seth believed every word of it. Now he felt not only fooled, but betrayed.

"Tell me, son. Did you put on sunscreen before coming out here?"

Seth looked over his shoulder and found Papa rolling up on his scooter. "No. Why?"

"Long as you've been out here, you're due for a nasty sunburn."

Seth looked up at the bland, gray sky. The sun was nowhere to be seen. "I really don't think--"

Papa rattled off a laugh and Seth fought the urge not to spit in his general direction.

"That was a joke," Seth said.

"Not my best material. Apologies."

Papa stopped his ride beside Seth. "I read your face clear as a newspaper headline."

"Yeah? What's the story?"

"You're upset. Disappointed"

Seth rolled his eyes. "Didn't exactly have to be psychic to figure that out."

"It's more than that though," Papa said. "Your ego has been wounded. And, hell, I don't blame you."

"I'm really tired of people saying that to me. *They don't blame me.* Why the hell would they? It wasn't my fucking fault that this happened to me. But now every decision that is made, is made with my disability in mind, isn't it?"

Papa sat patiently, listening to Seth.

"You told me things were going to be different here. But when it comes time to put some action behind those words you end up treating me like a cripple who isn't worth shit. You won't even give me a chance to prove that I can help and show the people here that I'm capable of contributing."

"There's the rub," Papa said. "You don't need to prove yourself. The community knows you're capable because I've told them about you.

"That talk we had yesterday, I meant all of it. You are meant for great things. Your purpose is far more meaningful than a food run that could be handled by a group of adequately trained chimpanzees." Papa adjusted himself in his seat, the vinyl making an awkward farting sound in the process. Seth held back a smirk.

"Franklin and Alexander are integral cogs in the machine. They're loyal and trustworthy. They're one hundred percent committed to the cause. And they follow commands without protest." Papa pointed a thick finger at Seth. "But you, Seth, you think about things. You question the reason behind why I make decisions. That is a worthwhile attribute. One that cannot be taught."

Seth sat a little taller in his chair. He had felt like a child throwing a fit only moments ago, but Papa's words calmed his temper. "So, what are you saying?"

"I have no need for another Yes Man, or a mouthpiece. What I need, my son, is a free thinker. Someone worthy and capable of carrying on and leading after I'm gone. I don't know if you've noticed, but I ain't the picture of health these days." As if to prove his point, he coughed up a mouthful of phlegm which he spat into his palm. He examined the mass before shaking it off onto the ground. Seth noticed that blood was intermixed with the mucus.

"But I thought--"

"You thought it was all in Yahweh's plan, right?" Papa cast a wink. "I wasn't always the man you see before you. I was healthier than your brother even. I suppose, back then, we all were. But things change. Sometimes for the worse, and sometimes for the better."

Seth watched the man's gaze drift into the desert as he told his story.

CHAPTER 16

"I wasn't always so fat I could barely walk. Didn't have these..." He gestured lazily to the sores and scars on his face. "Malformities. Don't get me wrong, I wasn't movie star handsome, but I was married. Had two kids. If you can believe that."

Seth wouldn't have guessed it, but he supposed that's why Papa said he was a different man before all of this.

"I wasn't a leader back then, but I had a knack for connecting with people. My mother, Yahweh rest her soul, said I was born with the gift of gab and that got me through some lean years."

"You weren't always a preacher?"

Papa chuckled. "No. I worked in customer service which, all things considered, isn't all that different. It's all about listening, you see. Making people know you're hearing them. Good or bad. The key to people is making them believe you care. That you're on their side. And I was. It wasn't God's work, necessarily, but it was honest."

Papa placed his hands against the armrests and with considerable effort, forced himself into a standing position. The effort left him short of breath and soaking in perspiration. He pulled his slacks away from his crotch and shifted uncomfortably on his feet. "That damn vinyl gets my taint all sweaty." He raised his hands toward the sky and looked to the gray nothingness. "My kingdom for some Gold Bond."

Listening to the old man complain about his moist genitals wasn't how Seth wanted the conversation to go but he made the rare wise decision to keep his mouth closed. Eventually Papa returned his attention to him.

"I was at work when the bombs started falling. It was panic unlike anything I'd seen before or have seen since. I tried to drive home but the highways were jammed. So, you know what I did? I ran. Almost seven miles. It was a miracle I didn't have a coronary, but I didn't. I made it home to my wife and my boys. And the house was unharmed. I knew when I saw it my family was okay, and I thought I was destined to take them away to safety."

Seth saw tears in Papa's eyes, a sight that made him even more uncomfortable than talk of his sweaty taint. He considered telling him he didn't have to go on but understood this was a tale he needed to hear.

"I barely made it through the front door when the second wave of bombs hit. Next thing I knew I was on the other side of the street staring at what remained of my house. And let me tell you son, it wasn't much. A few bits of siding. Chunks of smashed wood. But it was my home!"

Tears streamed down his scared face and the man made no effort to wipe them away. His eyes had turned cherry red and snot bubbled from his right nostril. Seth wouldn't allow himself to look away.

"I found them in the rubble. Their broken and burned bodies. I swear, I can still smell their flesh cooking. It was beyond my worst nightmares. My life had turned into a horror story and I was helpless. All I could do was stand there and watch the flames eat away at their remains."

"The bombs put out my family. I should have been, too and that infuriated me. So, I walked into that fire to be with them again. In death if not in life." His fingers subconsciously dragged across his scarred face.

"I woke up, days later. And the first thing I saw was the pastor that had rescued me. He said it was a miracle. And he was right."

"But your whole family died. How can that be a miracle?"

"Oh, believe me. I thought the same thing then. But over time, he taught me about Yahweh. About the love He has for us. It was in the subsequent months spent with that man, as he helped me recover physically and mentally, that I knew what I had to do. Gerald, the pastor, and I became quite the team. And we saved others in the same way he had saved me. Body and soul."

Papa was short of breath. Seth wasn't sure whether it was due to exertion from standing or from the long, rambling speech. The man returned to his scooter and sat.

"Eventually, we ended up here. And we built this place so others could join us and be a part of something good again."

"What happened to him?" Seth asked.

"After a while, Gerald felt called to move on. He realized his mission was to find others adrift in this sea of chaos and to save them." Papa looked to the casino and smiled. "So here we are, honoring the memory of my friend."

"He's dead?" Seth asked.

"I choose to believe he is not. Nothing would warm my heart more than to know he's out there, spreading Yahweh's love to those less fortunate than ourselves."

Papa used the scooter's joystick to make a one quarter turn. The angle gave Seth his best look ever at the festering sores on the man's face. They looked infected and angry and red streaks trailed down his neck before disappearing under his shirt. Seth realized the man's condition was more dire than he'd initially thought.

"Gerald raised me up from the ashes to become Yahweh's vessel. Now I must do the same for you." Papa rested his hand atop Seth's forearm and gave it a firm squeeze. "You are the future, my child."

Papa removed his hand and drove the scooter to the casino.

"Seth?" Papa called.

He turned to look at the man who was half in, half out of the building. "Yes?"

"Why don't you come up to my room in about thirty minutes. I'd like to introduce you to someone. Someone I think you'll quite enjoy meeting."

Seth had never felt so much trust put on him before. Not from his parents. Not from Wyatt. Not from Trooper. Yet here was a great man, maybe the greatest he had ever met, telling him that he was not only special, but chosen. His arms erupted in goosebumps and he unleashed the grin he'd been holding back.

CHAPTER 17

WYATT MOVED WITH ALEXANDER'S CREW AS THEY APPROACHED a few ramshackle buildings which stood in stark contrast to the flat land around them. Burying the bodies of their own had put them more than two hours behind schedule.

The act of putting the dead in the ground was awkward for Wyatt, who hadn't known them. The others in the group shared anecdotes and stories of better times as they shared their grief, leaving Wyatt feeling like a fly on the wall observing private, secret events to which he shouldn't have been privy. He wondered how long it would take for him to shake that feeling of being an intruder in their midst, then thought that might never happen.

The realization that he was with others but still alone hit him harder than he'd expected, and he'd spent much of the subsequent journey separated and inside his head. He knew he was expecting too much too fast. These people had spent months, even years together. He'd been there mere hours. But the isolation, coupled with the brief but bloody battle, had made him question why he wanted to come out here in the first place.

Would he even stop being stupid?

As they neared the land on which the hermit lived, Wyatt thought that it might easily be overlooked if you didn't know it was there. The buildings were coated in mud and debris. At a distance, they'd looked like random bumps in the earth. It was a sloppy, yet effective, camouflage and wholly different from the casino which may as well have still flaunted neon lights while someone on a loudspeaker beckoned, 'Come on in!'

Between the two, he thought the hermit might have the better idea.

Alexander had been in the lead and now he turned to face his people. "Everyone knows the drill here except you, Wyatt. Follow in my footsteps. Don't deviate so much as an inch. This place is booby-trapped out the ass. Got it?" He didn't wait for an answer before proceeding ahead.

So much for thinking he had any input. He was just another mindless grunt. Wyatt took a look back at the two men who hauled the wagon which held not only a variety of electronic gadgets, but also the injured cannibal. He found the boy's eyes, which were half-open and delirious.

One of the soldiers saw Wyatt staring and snickered. "Don't worry. Your butt buddy's alive. For now," the soldier said.

Wyatt looked away. He supposed he deserved their scorn. After all, he was the reason they had the extra workload. The reason they were carting around someone that killed their friends. The reason the cannibal was still alive.

For now, anyway.

A balding, middle aged man named Zak had cleaned the cannibal's wounds with water, slapped on a 4x4 bandage, and taped it fast. At first Wyatt thought Zak to be kind. Then he saw the man grab the kid by the balls and squeeze hard enough to turn his knuckles white. The injured boy writhed in pain while Zak cackled like a giddy hen.

Wyatt considered speaking up in protest but knew that would be unwise. Unwise? Hell, it would have been so fucking dumb it might have got him shot too. So, he stayed silent.

He followed behind Alexander, leaving barely a yard between the two of them. They stepped toward a low fence that was hand-made from sticks and sagebrush and, Wyatt thought, wouldn't have discouraged a determined prairie dog.

As Alexander took a step over it, Wyatt noticed metal glint under his legs and saw a blade protruding from the debris.

Alexander looked at him over his shoulder. "Like I said. Booby trapped out the ass.".

"I see," Wyatt said in disbelief.

"This guy knows his shit. Crazy, but crazy smart, too."

The fence was one of the more well-built structures on the property. Ahead were three buildings, all in various states of disrepair. Only, upon closer inspection, Wyatt thought they'd never been *in* repair.

The main shack was leaning at a fifteen-degree angle and didn't look capable of resisting a strong breeze. A greenhouse, of sorts, was cobbled together from assorted plastic and tape, all domed together to make a large sized igloo. The other building, maybe a supply shed Wyatt thought, was a cross between a broom closet and teepee.

Alexander stopped a few yards before the structures, cupped his hands to his mouth and did his best impression of a crow.

Kaw. Kaw.

That wasn't half-bad, Wyatt thought.

Twenty seconds of silence followed and then Alexander spoke. "We'd like to trade. Have some merchandise that might interest you."

Wyatt wondered who the hell was he talking to and followed Alexander's gaze to the shed. He saw light reflect off glass and, after a moment, realized he was looking at binoculars hidden amongst the menagerie of junk.

The reflection vanished and then a door made of pallet wood and vines swung open. Behind it was a black hole.

Wyatt waited, nervous to see who might emerge, and his fingers tightened around the rifle. He shifted on his feet and the noise drew Alexander's attention.

"Hold still. And don't so much as twitch that AK or we're all dead."

"Uh, sure." Wyatt stopped fidgeting, now afraid to move. He did his best impression of a statue for what felt like an eternity before a figure emerged from the darkness.

The white hair caught his attention first. A wild mane of it surrounded a small, pinched face that was etched with wrinkles deep enough to get lost in. An equally unkempt snow-colored beard covered the bottom half of that face while somewhere in the midst laid beady eyes and a ski-slope nose. Wyatt presumes a mouth was there too but couldn't see it through the forest of follicles.

The hermit stepped into the open, bent at the waist like he was carrying an invisible anvil on his back. Despite his advanced age and poor posture, Wyatt was downright shocked to see that the man looked healthy and well fed. How was that possible in the middle of this vast nothingness?

He moved toward the soldiers, not bothering with greetings or small talk or even polite nods. His course took him straight to the cart which he leaned over and peered into. When he saw the injured cannibal, his face darkened, and he finally spoke.

"Got no use for that," he said to Alexander.

"Ran into some trouble along the way." Alexander motioned to the men who'd been handling the cart. "Get that out of there."

The men grabbed onto the boy's arms, caring little that he was shot and maybe near death as they jerked him from the wagon and dropped him onto the ground. A low, tired groan escaped his lips, but he made no effort to move.

With that out of the way, the hermit rummaged through the goods. There were computers and cell phones. Batteries by the bucketload. Motors big and small. Assorted wires and transistors and cables that Wyatt imagined would have given the average Radio Shack nerd a hard-on, but he saw no use for such things now and couldn't imagine why the hermit would have any interest in the pile of junk.

The man hummed as he sifted through the lot of it, separating it into two piles. One was quite large, outpacing the other rapidly. As he sorted the goods, he shot a glance at Wyatt.

"Got yourself a new guy there. He know what he signed up for?"

Wyatt turned his attention to Alexander, wondering what that was about, but the man ignored him.

"You interested or not?" Alexander asked the hermit.

"Lord, you have the patience of a meerkat on cocaine, Alexander. You'd think you could humor such an aged gentleman. Especially one who you depend on for nutritional needs." He looked from the junk to Alexander. "Tell me. How does your garden grow?"

Alexander's nostrils flared but he remained silent.

"Not well, I see. Not well at all."

He continued splitting the goods up, not speaking again until he was finished. Then he motioned to the large pile. "I'll accept this. The rest..." He motioned to the smaller pile, which was mostly electrical cords and various plastic pieces. "Is trash. I'd think by now you'd know the difference between useful and useless but alas, I expect too much from a bunch of aspiring jarheads."

He spun on his heels and walked toward the greenhouse. "You wait where you are. I buried a landmine somewhere in the vicinity last month, but I'll be damned if I can remember the precise location. Better I go boom than the lot of you."

He disappeared into the plastic dome and Wyatt took the opportunity to speak up. He leaned into Alexander and whispered. "What's the deal with this guy?"

"Not much to say," Alexander said, keeping his eyes forward. "There are useful people outside the walls, but there are no friends out here."

"What about me? My family?"

Alexander lifted an eyebrow. "That's different. You were passing through. People like the hermit, they live in isolation for a reason. Not fit for communal living."

Wyatt knew this was true. His time on the road had shown him that people out here were dangerous at best, deadly at worst. "Then why do you trust him?"

Alexander shrugged his shoulders. "Our relationship is symbiotic. We gather things he needs when we explore the cities. He helps us out when supplies run low. But know one thing, the hermit needs us far more than we need him. And he understands that."

The hermit emerged from the greenhouse pushing a rusty wheelbarrow. When he got closer Wyatt saw it was filled with vegetables. Most were green and leafy. Lettuce, cabbage, Brussel sprouts, celery. But there were also carrots, beets, radishes, and squash.

"Here you go. Should last you a spell unless you get glutinous."

The hermit sat the wheelbarrow at Wyatt's feet and the smell of the fresh food had his mouth watering. He wanted to see what other gold awaited and began exploring. There were turnips and peas and, he thought, rutabagas. He pushed into the wheelbarrow for a better look, only to catch his palm on a rusty shard of metal that poked from one of the wagon's many holes.

"Fuck." He retracted his hand as blood oozed from the cut.

Clark barked out a derisive chortle. "Survive a gunfight and get attacked by a wheelbarrow. Classic."

"I'll get some antiseptic," the hermit said as he retreated to the shack.

"Fucking moron," Laurie said, and the group shared a laugh at Wyatt's expense.

"Enough," Alexander said. He looked at Wyatt's sliced palm and pulled a handkerchief from his pocket. "When we get back to the casino tomorrow, you go straight to medical. I don't need you getting an infection."

That was the last thing Wyatt wanted too. He'd heard the horror stories about tetanus and, as far as he could remember, his last vaccine was over ten years ago. He wondered how long they remained viable as he blotted blood from his hand with the cloth.

"What about tonight?" Wyatt asked.

"We spend tonight in there." He motioned to the larger building. It was about six feet wide by twenty feet long and Wyatt couldn't imagine spending the night in such tight quarters with these people who had such a low opinion of him. But he's already defied Alexander once today and wasn't about to make that mistake again.

CHAPTER 18

SPREAD OUT ON THE BATHROOM VANITY WAS A VARIETY OF makeup the women of the community had gathered and given Barb as part of a welcome gift. She appreciated the gesture, but as her attention drifted from the various products to the reflection of her mangled face, the more she wondered if it was some sort of cruel joke.

After all, what good was makeup when half your face looked like it had been run through a meat grinder? People always joked about putting makeup on a pig but at least pigs had two good eyes.

She grabbed a tube of mascara, unscrewed it, and sighed as she examined the brush. It was the same brand she'd used at home and wasn't cheap. The bristles were clean and fresh, not gunked up.

What the hell, she thought. She was alone in her room. No one was going to laugh at her for trying to beautify the pig.

The mascara went on smooth, just like the good old days. When that was finished, she took the eyeliner, gliding it around. She then covered the scars with her hand and examined her better half in the mirror.

Barbara was never vain, but she'd always taken care of herself.

Had always believed that making a good impression meant looking presentable. Seeing herself with makeup again for the first time in years was startling and, to her surprise, pleasing. "Not too bad for an old broad," she said.

But then she removed her hand. The difference was so jarring, so hideous, that a wave of self-loathing washed over her, and tears spilled from her remaining eye and down her cheek. The freshly applied makeup went along for the ride, making the situation even worse.

And then someone knocked on her hotel room door.

"Fuck!" She muttered.

She searched the vanity for tissues but found none so she grabbed a hand towel and dragged it across her stained face, trying to remove the foundation so whoever was banging on her door wouldn't see her looking like a disfigured clown.

Another knock. Why were these people so damned persistent?

"Coming!"

She tossed the towel aside and went to the door, caring little about what kind of impression she made and eager to ask whoever was out there if they'd ever heard of privacy.

When Barbara unlatched the safety chain and spun the handle, in the perfect frame of mind to go on a rant, only to find Richard's smiling face.

Her annoyance vanished, replaced with flustered shock.

"Did I run you from the loo?" He asked. "I apologize if I did."

She shook her head. "No." But what was she supposed to say she was doing? Trying to make herself look less deformed? That was the truth, but she wasn't about to say it aloud. "I was just... reading."

She prayed he didn't ask her what it was that she was reading as her frazzled mind would have been unable to summon a lie. Much to her relief, he didn't follow up on it.

Instead, he was kind and that was even worse. "Are you alright, Barbara?"

"Fine. I'm fine."

"Forgive me for saying so but you don't look it."

She could only imagine how awful she looked. If a bag had been nearby, she'd have pulled it over her head. Instead the brief facade of having her shit together imploded. She sobbed openly as the culmination of everything and everyone she lost became too much to push deep inside and ignore.

"Do you want me to go?" But even as Richard asked the question, she felt his hands on her shoulders. They were firm, reassuring.

"I'm sorry," she said. "I'm such a fucking disaster."

"I don't believe that for a second." His fingers massaged her shoulders. "Why don't you sit down and as me mum always said, 'Take a load off.'

Barbara sat on the edge of the bed. Richard didn't join her, but he stayed close by, protective.

"You don't have to stay," she said.

"I know. But I want to. If you'll have me."

She couldn't understand why he was being so nice to her. "Why would you want to be around some scarred-up hag like me?"

"Come now," Richard said. "If you want to get me right mad, you'll keep going on about yourself all negative like that."

"It's the truth."

"So, you've got a nick on your face. What's that matter in the grand plan of things?"

A nick, she thought. If it was only a nick, she could bear to look at herself. This was a deformity.

"It matters a lot."

"So, says you. But I disagree and there's nothing you can say that'll change my mind."

She realized he wasn't just offering platitudes. That he really meant it. And that made her want to start crying all over again. "Can you really look at me and tell me I'm not hideous?"

Richard crouched down so they were at face level. "Barbara, you're not hideous. There, I said it. And it's the truth. Now can we move on?"

"I suppose."

"Good." He held up a bottle of wine he'd brought with him. "I thought maybe we could have a drink. It's a full bodied petite sirah. And I'll confess I have not a clue what that means but Myrtle told me it was quite tasty and, well, here I am."

That made Barbara forget about her embarrassment and laugh. "Here you are." She glanced around her room, which wasn't exactly set up for guests. "I'd invite you to stay but..."

Richard shook his head. "There's a mezzanine on the third floor. It doesn't overlook much of anything but it's private and I've always been fond of the night air. Won't you join me?"

How could she resist?

CHAPTER 19

NIGHT IN THE HERMIT'S GUEST HOUSE WAS DULL AND uneventful with the other soldiers ignoring Wyatt. Their attitudes hadn't changed on the trek back to the casino with only Alexander bothering to make occasional small talk with him.

The rest of the men and women made no effort to hide the fact that they were done with Wyatt, for the time being. Maybe even forever. That was just as well because he too looked forward to a break. But first he needed to help Alexander take the wounded cannibal to the medical bay.

They tied the boy onto a wheeled office chair. The kid wavered between semi-conscious and delirious. He never spoke but an occasional groan slipped from his dry, cracked lips.

They took a back entrance, then traversed a series of industrial, barren hallways which had obviously been staff only areas before the world fell apart.

Things were silent for a while, but Wyatt eventually worked up the nerve to ask Alexander the question that had been gnawing away at him for the past day. "Am I going to be punished?"

Alexander gave him a sideways glance. "Why would you think that?"

"Why don't you answer my question?"

Alexander flashed a brief grin, but it was enough to allay some of Wyatt's nerves. "I didn't intend to be cryptic. I just thought you understood this place better than that. We don't punish people. You aren't going to get detention or send to your room with no supper."

He meant supper as in the meal, but the word made Wyatt wonder how his dog was doing. He missed that mutt. "Okay. Thanks."

"No need to thank me. I told you before, we're good people. That means we're fair."

"I know. I didn't mean it like I was doubting you. I guess, when you yelled at me, I just got a little worried that I ruined everything."

"No. Most of that was the heat of the battle. You know, endorphins and adrenaline and that crap. I was harder than I meant to be." He winked. "But don't disobey me again."

Wyatt grinned. "I don't plan too."

"Good."

They came to a door with a cross painted in white. Alexander pulled a ring of keys from his waistband and unlocked it, then pushed the chair holding the cannibal into a large room that contained nothing but empty gurneys and beds.

Alexander pushed a button on the inside of the doorway and waited.

"You guys even have a doctor?" Wyatt asked.

"Sort of. She was a veterinarian. I'm not saying I'd trust her with major surgery, but she's pretty great."

Wyatt was impressed. This place really did have everything.

Footfalls clicked against the tile floor, approaching them, and a moment later Ramona Sidaris came into the room. She wore a lab coat over scrubs, a small pair of spectacles, and had long gray hair which was pulled into a ponytail. Wyatt thought she was at least sixty.

"What mess did you bring me this time, Alexander?" Her tone was husky, a smoker's voice.

"Oh, little of this. Little of that."

When Ramona got close enough to see the cannibal tied to the chair, Wyatt expected surprise or horror on her face, but if she felt either she hid it well. "This isn't one of ours."

Alexander shook his head. "Nope. He was a stray and Wyatt decided to bring him home."

Ramona looked at Wyatt and raised an eyebrow. "I take it you're Wyatt?"

He nodded.

"Not too bright, are you?"

Wyatt was unsure whether she expected an answer or if it was sarcasm and decided to stay quiet.

Ramona squatted down in front of the cannibal and peeled back the bandage. The gunshot wound was red and oozed a milky, yellow pus. Wyatt was three feet away but could smell it.

"And who put this boy in such a miserable condition?" Ramona stood.

Alexander tipped his head toward Wyatt.

"Next time you shoot someone, make it a kill shot. It's kinder, I assure you."

Wyatt felt his stomach tighten. "Is he going to die?"

The woman looked down on the boy and her mouth twisted sideways as she considered it. "Too soon to tell. I'm a doctor, not a psychic."

She turned away from them, heading back the way she came.

"Wyatt also needs a tetanus shot," Alexander called to her.

"They still have those?" Wyatt asked.

Alexander shrugged. "That's what she says it is. Burns like hell. For all I really know she injects you with rubbing alcohol, but whatever it is, it seems to work."

Wyatt remembered his last tetanus shot. His arm was so sore he missed two days of school. The thought or getting another didn't thrill him but he wasn't about to admit that to Alexander.

"I need to go tell Franklin and Papa about the men we lost. And your little hero move," Alexander said.

Wyatt cringed.

"Think you can stay out of trouble?"

"I'll try."

"There's a thought."

Alexander left and Wyatt heard the door lock behind him. He waited, shifting back and forth on his tired feet for what felt like an eternity. With nothing to do, boredom and curiosity got the better of him and he began wandering around the room, which carried the pungent aroma of antiseptic.

On the counters were the expected first aid products. Bandages, gauze, tongue depressors, gloves. Nothing unique enough to hold his interest. He moved on to metal cabinets which lined the opposite wall. He tried the latch on the first, only to find it locked. Tried the second with the same lack of results.

Already exhausted from the trek back to the casino, he considered sprawling on one of the beds and catching a few winks until the doctor returned, but before Wyatt could put his ass on the mattress the cannibal spoke.

"You got a name?"

Wyatt spun so fast he almost lost his balance. The boy's eyes were red and wild, but he was alert for the first time since Wyatt shot him. "I'm Wyatt."

"Where the hell am I?" He shifted as much as the ropes would allow, which wasn't much at all. Movement caused his face to contort into a grimace.

"Somewhere safe," Wyatt said as he moved to him.

"I doubt that."

"Why?"

"I was free in the desert. Now I'm tied up like a calf getting hauled to the slaughterhouse."

"You're fine," Wyatt said. "The rope's for our safety."

"Fuck man, you shot me. How am I the dangerous one?"

It annoyed Wyatt that the boy thought he could get away with playing the victim. "Your asshole people killed my friends."

Friends were an exaggeration. He still hadn't bothered to learn the names of the fallen, but the point was still true.

"And how many of mine did you kill?"

Rather than continue the debate, Wyatt decided to end the conversation. "It doesn't matter. I made sure you stayed alive. And we brought you back here to get fixed up."

The fight seemed to have left the boy too. He slumped back in the chair, the motion causing so much pain tears leaked from his eyes.

Wyatt wanted to do something to ease his misery, then remembered that he was in the medical bay. There must be painkillers somewhere, even if it was just aspirin. Anything would be better than nothing.

Until he could find something, he tried to distract the kid. "I told you my name, but you didn't reciprocate."

Wyatt tried an Army green metal cabinet. It was locked. Tried another. Also locked.

"Vern," he said. "What did you say yours was?"

Wyatt looked back at the boy who was fading fast. "Wyatt."

"That's right." He moaned. "You gonna kill me, Wyatt?"

"No."

"You sure?"

"I am. The doc here is going to make you good as new. Except you'll have a nasty scar and a cool story to tell for the rest of your life."

Vern half-smiled at that. "That's good. I think I'm thirteen but might've lost count. I want to see what it's like to get old." His eyelids fell shut and the last words came out in a mumble, "Never thought I'd have that chance..."

Wyatt fiddled with a lock, spinning the dial to and fro as if he had the world's best luck and would stumble across the combination when--

"Is there a reason you're trying to break into the supply closet?"

He spun around and found Ramona Sidaris staring at him from across the room. He looked to Vern who had slipped back into unconsciousness.

"Um... No?"

She moved toward him, and he saw the syringe in her hand. Instinctively he stepped away from the door, closer to one of the hospital beds, and eased onto it.

"Why's it locked?" He asked.

Ramona surprised him by smiling. Her teeth were stained nicotine beige, but she appeared sincere. "To keep people from stealing our limited supplies."

To prove her point, she opened the lock, removed it, then pulled the door open. Inside were dozens of small vials, all organized in perfect rows.

"Are vaccines a hot ticket on the black market or something?" He asked. "I mean, if it was like morphine or something I could understand, but are people really breaking down doors to make sure they don't get polio?"

"You're kind of special, aren't you?" she asked. Wyatt knew she was being polite and not calling him a dumbass straight to his face.

"That's what my mom says," he said, offering an apologetic grin.

"Well, Wyatt, since you need things spelled out. No. I don't suspect our people would be apt to raid my meager supplies. But if less savory characters should ever gain entry." She looked to the cannibal. "Let's just say I prefer to be safe than sorry."

He really was an idiot and felt the blood flood his cheeks in embarrassment. "I'm usually not so paranoid. But I guess I saw everything locked and then that door and..."

Ramona took a vial, then closed the door and padlocked it. "And you assumed that something sinister was going on. Because of a locked door. Remind me to never take a shit around you unless I want you to burst inside and verify that I'm doing nothing more harmful than wiping my own ass."

Wyatt knew he was only digging himself a deeper hole and annoying yet another person who wielded some semblance of power here. He stood up. "You know, I think I'll just grab a band aid and leave you alone."

"Wait," Ramona said with an exasperated exhale. "Why does Alexander think you need a tetanus shot anyway?"

He held his hand out. She grabbed it and removed the blood-soaked and dirt-covered handkerchief it was wrapped in. "Cut it on a rusty wheelbarrow."

"That'll do it," she said. "Drop your drawers and bend over."

Wyatt froze.

"It's okay. I'm a doctor."

"Can't you give it to me in my arm?"

Ramona smirked. "I'm an old woman, Wyatt. The pleasures I get in life these days are small. And the last time I saw an ass as firm as yours appears to be was ages ago. Humor me. Please."

He sighed and unbuckled his belt.

CHAPTER 20

WYATT HOPED TO RETURN TO HIS ROOM AND GET CLEANED UP without seeing anyone else. He needed time to prepare his story, to figure out what he was going to say to the others. And besides that, his ass hurt.

He would have stayed in the medical bay longer, but Ramona made it clear he was fine to leave and assured him she would take care of the cannibal aka Vern. So, rather than linger and continue making a fool of himself, he left staying close to the walls his head bowed. All the while he kept an eye out for his mother as the last thing he wanted was her to making a big fuss about why he was limping, where he'd gone, and what happened.

The closer he got to his room, the more optimistic he felt. Right now, there was nothing better than having alone time to process his thoughts and heal. He dug through his pockets for the room key when--

"Wyatt?"

His shoulders slumped, but he didn't turn around. If he was quick enough maybe he could make a clean getaway. He found the key was in a back pocket, pulled it out, and swiped it against the lock.

"Wyatt, don't you hear me?"

Yes, he thought, but I don't want to do this yet.

Then Allie was at his side. He could breathe in her delicate, floral scent and as much as he wanted - needed - to be alone, her very presence was intoxicating. As much as he wanted to take her in his arms, to take her to bed, that would cause more problems than it would solve.

He pushed the door and held it open, still not responding to her. It was a dick move and he knew that but what was he supposed to say?

"What's wrong?" She followed him into the room, circling around and forcing him to make eye contact. He wasn't trying to ignore her; he just couldn't find a way to tell the story that wouldn't bring about unneeded drama.

"Just got a tetanus shot."

"A tetanus shot?" She asked. "Why?"

He limped towards the bed and eased on the edge. It felt like he was sitting atop a flaming baseball and he did his best to hide his discomfort.

"While we were out. I cut my hand. On a wheelbarrow."

Allie blinked fast in confusion. "I have too many questions."

Wyatt sighed. "We went to see a man who gave us fresh food. It was all in a wheelbarrow. There was a sharp bit of metal, the rusty kind of course and..." He showed her the freshly dressed wound. "I ended up with a shot in my butt."

"Jesus." Allie whispered and moved to him. She enveloped his injured hand with her own.

Wyatt let her examine it. She looked up at him, but his eyes had found another spot on the ground to stare at.

"And what else? You're hiding something."

He could feel her heartbeat speeding up in her fingertips. She was onto him and there was no sense holding back further. Time to dive into the deep end.

"When we were on the way there, we lost three guys. Some cannibals started shooting at us--"

"Shooting?" Allie exclaimed.

"Well, not shooting. They were throwing spears. Came out of nowhere." He felt her squeeze his bandaged hand tighter. "We shot back. It was chaos. And I shot a guy. They-- Alexander wanted me to kill him, but I... I said we should bring him back instead; in case he has information we could use. So, he's here."

Wyatt said the last sentence barely above a whisper. Everything came out all at once, and yet, there was so much more he wanted to say. How he'd disappointed Alexander and felt like he failed some test of courage. Of loyalty. How the others all hated him.

"So, the cannibals that killed some of Alexander's men. The cannibals who were trying to kill you. You saved one of them? And brought him here?" Allie's shoulders dropped and disapproval clouded her face, but she didn't let his hand go.

"He's in the medical bay. Barely conscious. I think he's more scared of us than we are of--"

"Stop. I know you haven't forgotten what they did to your brother. To Pete. What they would have done to us." She paused. They both knew where she was going. Time to twist the knife. Rub salt in the wound. "Do I have to remind you what happened to Trooper?"

"Allie, he's a boy. A kid. Maybe not even a teenager yet."

She shook her head to deny that meant anything. Wyatt now looked her in the eyes. There was no shame in his conviction that he had made the right choice.

"A savage is a savage no matter its age." She dropped his hand. Not in anger or even overt rudeness. It was more like letting loose of an objectionable object. A slimy fish. Or a pile of dog shit. "You know better than this. That thing being here, inside here, with all of us, puts everyone in danger."

"The kid can barely move. He'll be strapped into a hospital bed for the next month getting treated for the gunshot wounds I put in his body. If he lives at all." Wyatt raised his voice to match Allie's. They were getting close to an argument, the very opposite of what he wanted right now. "And what happened before... You can't judge all of them just because of the actions of a few."

"Jesus Christ, Wyatt! He's a goddamn cannibal. He eats people!" She said. "What makes you think he's any different from the others. Did he tell you what he wants to be when he grows up? Maybe invite you back to his place for an afternoon snack. If he did, who was--"

A loud crack interrupted her. They both stopped and listened for the announcement to come over the speakers.

"Attention friends. Everyone is to return to their rooms for the remainder of the day. A special announcement and demonstration will take place at the front of the casino tomorrow morning at eight a.m. Your presence is required. Have a blessed evening."

Damn it, Wyatt thought. The voice didn't sound any more or less cheerful than it did when announcing a meal, but he knew whatever was going to happen in the front hall probably had to do with the outing. And his gut told him it wasn't good.

Allie practically bounced off the bed and out of the room without another word. Wyatt wondered if she was that eager to be away from him or if she was really that subservient to the omnipotent, anonymous voice in the sky. He almost preferred the former because the Allie he knew, the Allie he loved, couldn't be that much of a follower.

Could she?

CHAPTER 21

Sleep had been impossible, both due to nerves and the throbbing in his butt. The pain was less this morning. No more flaming hot baseball in his right cheek, just an angry bump. He was out of bed before the pathetic excuse for sunrise and expected to be one of the first to the lobby, but he was wrong.

Everyone was there. Not just the main gaggle of geese. *Everyone.*

They were lined up like teenage girls before a boyband concert, chatting and nattering like giddy hens. And one by one they funneled outside. Being amongst them was about as high on Wyatt's *Things I Want to Do* list as getting a jalapeno enema, but he allowed himself to be dragged along for the ride.

Papa was already in the middle of his speech. Wyatt couldn't see him yet and the sound was muffled by the doors, but the man's voice rose above the din of the crowd as he preached about God.

As Wyatt neared the entrance he could gather bits and pieces of the sermon, and it occurred to him that these people, living in an oasis of their own making after the wars, probably saw their fortune as a gift hand delivered by God himself.

He couldn't blame them. But even though he had just as much

reason to be grateful he wasn't sure how much religion had to do with his circumstances.

Through the smoked glass Wyatt took in the scene. Papa stood on a large platform, outside of the gates which stood open, allowing a clear view. His guards were planted on the platform with him and Wyatt noticed that both now held AKs. But they weren't looking in the same direction as Papa, which was at the growing crowd. They peered into the desert.

Then, as Wyatt looked closer, he had to stop himself from swearing out loud. Seth was on the platform with Papa and he wore the biggest shit-eating grin Wyatt had ever seen as a stunning, buxom woman sat at his side. Their body language insinuated that they weren't just sharing space. They were together.

Just as he began to wonder how exactly Seth had managed to get in this coveted position so quickly, and who the woman was, Wyatt noticed an object at the rear of the platform. There stood a tall, wooden structure and affixed to it was an object wrapped in a white tarp.

It looked like a marshmallow. As Wyatt stared, trying to make sense of it, he thought it moved.

Even though Papa was speaking, a murmur ran through the crowd like a babbling brook. Everyone was muttering, whispering, speculating. Wyatt gathered bits and pieces, enough to realize they were as clueless as himself.

A wave of applause followed as Papa finished making a statement about the glory of Yahweh. As the noise silenced, a cry came from one end of the throng.

"Show us, Papa!"

"We want to see!"

The yells were answered with more applause, but Papa chuckled and raised his hand to silence his people.

"Alright... Alright." Everyone hushed quickly. "Let us not forget the old saying. 'Good things come to those who wait.'"

Wyatt's eyes drifted over to Seth, who watched Papa with the avid eyes of a wolf as the woman at his side rubbed his shoulder. Wyatt thought she looked less enamored with Papa than most here. She looked in the man's general direction, but it was clear that was for show. At least, that was Wyatt's read on her.

"For anyone who isn't yet aware," Papa shifted on his feet, visibly tiring. Immediately some chuckles erupted. He knew the community well, and how fast word spread inside the casino walls. "Our protectors recently went out on a mission to procure a trade. Let's take a moment to recognize their work."

A woman from the crowd screamed over applause and cheers. "Alexander, we love you!"

Some started to chant, but Papa put his hand up and their words faded away.

"Indeed. These men and women make sacrifices for us, for our home. They do things most of us couldn't do.

"On this mission they encountered another group that seemed to need help, and Alexander and his team tried their best to show them the glory of Yahweh. To help them understand that it's only by working together that people can survive. Instead of listening and accepting the help..." Papa slowed down, and a hush immediately fell over the crowd. "Our protectors were attacked. And sadly, we lost three valued and trusted members of our community."

The crowd gasped. A few shouted, cried, wailed.

"The risks were great, but they accepted them because of their love for you." Papa continued speaking slowly, but his voice rose again in praise. "Every time our protectors go out, they know the danger. They understand they might be forced to make the ultimate sacrifice for the greater good."

The melancholy seemed to be spreading but Papa put a quick end to that. "Lest we despair, know that our protectors won the battle! And they killed the cannibals. The evildoers who dared attack the children of Yahweh!"

The crowd erupted, cheers, chants, and cries. Papa let it go on for a moment longer than was appropriate, but watching his face, Wyatt could see a faint grin. This was the reaction he wanted. He'd played the crowd like a Stradivarius.

The story wasn't close to the truth, of course. Maybe that was for the best as, selfishly, it concealed knowledge of his own role in the debacle. So, he stopped himself from shaking his head at the exaggerations. At how Papa propped up the protectors who were scared and taken by surprise. No one here needed to know that religion had nothing to do with it. At least, that's what Wyatt tried to tell himself.

"Our protectors..." Papa waited for the last of the conversation to quell before continuing. "Our protectors faithfully carried out their duty to keep us safe and killed those cannibals. All except one."

With the gusto of a nightclub magician, Papa pulled the tarp down from the structure in one ungracious move. He wobbled and Wyatt thought the man might fall, but then his attention went up. Along with everyone else.

Vern, the boy he'd shot, the boy he'd fought to spare, was lashed to an X-shaped construction high above the crowd. His arms and legs were each secured to pieces of lumber. He wore only a dirty cloth around his waist, leaving his stomach exposed. His ribs and hipbones jutted out and seemed to point accusingly at Wyatt.

In a flash of confusion, Wyatt looked around, certain that someone in the crowd would somehow connect him to what was in front of them.

But no one did. They were too busy shrieking in a disparate cacophony of cheers and jeers. The sound reminded Wyatt of monkeys in a zoo losing their minds as the handler came around with their midday snacks.

Wyatt eased into the darkness behind the crowd and stayed perfectly still. He wasn't going to cheer, but also wasn't going to risk being seen not cheering. He felt more pity for the boy now than he did after shooting him. And he knew that feeling, that empathy, was not shared by anyone else here today.

It was with sickening dread that Wyatt realized Vern was right after all; he'd never have the chance to get old.

Tears streamed down Vern's face, carving clean channels through the muddy filth. Wyatt wished he'd done something other than talk in those few seconds they were alone in the medical bay. Something to help. Something that mattered.

"Cannibals." Papa spat out. The crowd continued its cheer, now turning from glee to lust. "Deceivers!"

The crowd repeated the words, some of them shaking fists in anger.

"Vermin!" Papa raised both his palms into the air. "Sinners!" His usual strong, loud voice was a low growl, but still audible over the crowd. His southern drawl made it sound like a snake moving through tall grass.

"Please..." The boy gasped. "You don't get it. We're starving to death. My little sister, I watched her waste away to nothing but skin and bones. We need to eat. We--"

"You were coming here to take what we have!" Papa screamed, silencing him. "We are family! We are children of Yahweh! He is our father!" He pointed a fat finger at the boy. "Tell me, you miscreant, what kind of God do you follow because I know of none that allows you to steal and kill his children. To gobble us down and devour our souls."

Vern laid his head back against the board, his mouth open and slack. He remained silent.

"As I suspected. God-hating savages, the lot of you!" Papa reached under his podium and emerged with a sword. The blade was long and glistened even in the dim half-light of nuclear winter. It reminded Wyatt of something a Confederate general might wield. Custer or Jackson.

Vern saw it too. His eyes grew wide, two panicked white orbs against the grime of his flesh. Wyatt watched as the boy pulled at his restraints, tearing his own flesh in a vain attempt to free himself.

Without a hint of hesitation or remorse, Papa pushed the blade into Vern's side. The metal pierced under his rib cage, sinking deeper and deeper.

As a geyser of blood erupted from the wound, Vern shrieked, a noise that only increased the crowd's mania.

Wyatt stumbled backward. This bloodthirsty mob wasn't the community of people that was so eager to greet him and his family less than a week ago. Was there something in those hugs and handshakes that he missed? He wondered how they were able to hide such large fangs.

As he tried to find his mother and Allie in the crowd, to see if they fell on the side of madness or reason, he instead found Franklin holding a torch as he pushed his way through the men and women and to the platform. There, Franklin passed the torch to Papa like they were kicking off Hell's version of the Olympic Games.

Papa put his hand out and the obedient crowd went silent again.

"Any of those who intend us harm," Papa yelled out as if his voice could carry across the expanse outside of the casino boundaries. "Any who would refuse the truth, who refuse to acknowledge and accept Yahweh... You will find only immeasurable pain and death!"

And then, to Wyatt's growing horror, Papa turned and extended the torch to Seth. There was a moment of hesitation, a moment of hope for Wyatt, but Papa leaned into his brother and spoke words no one else could hear. Seth's face went blank and cold.

Seth pressed the torch to the wooden structure which, Wyatt realized, must have been coated in gas or oil as the fire raced across it lightning quick. The flames licked at Vern's feet, then his legs, then set afire the loincloth. Within seconds all of him was burning.

The boy unleashed a high-pitched wail like nothing Wyatt had ever heard.

Someone in the crowd began to chant Seth's name. More followed.

"Seth! Seth! Seth!"

Wyatt stared as his brother looked away from the flaming boy and to the audience. His expression, one of prideful accomplishment, scared Wyatt even more than the preceding horror.

It was all too much. Wyatt understood death earned in a fight.

Death served by a knife or a bullet. But he never imagined the revulsion of watching a human being burned alive. The sound of the flesh sizzling. Of the dying boy's screams descending into choked gurgles. The smell.

God, the smell was the worst. It wafted over the crowd like heavy fog and assaulted Wyatt's nose. Fought its way into his open mouth.

He could taste the char and smacked his lips shut, but damage had been done. His stomach lurched but, to his revulsion, it growled too. As if that instinctual, primordial part of his anatomy was unable to differentiate one cooking meat from another. And it wanted satiation. He hated himself.

"Let this be a warning!" Papa cried out again, nearly choking over the smoke covering the sky. "If you seek to do us harm, this..." He turned to the X, feasting his vengeful eyes on the burning center mass, on the boiling blood that leaked from it. "Is how your time on Earth will end. I pray this message reaches you. For Yahweh knows who his children are, and who will follow the true path."

Papa turned away from the fire, which rose higher and flame silhouetted him like an avenging angel.

Wyatt wanted no part of this. He continued his retreat until he collided with the glass doors and couldn't move anymore. Then he closed his eyes and prayed for it all to end.

CHAPTER 22

WYATT LAID ON HIS BED WITH SUPPER BY HIS SIDE. HIS ROUGH fur felt good, comforting. And he'd missed that because next to Trooper, Supper was his best friend. Even though the dog wouldn't be able to answer any of his questions from the morning. From the demonstration.

"Jesus." Wyatt whispered and scratched the dog's ear as a memory of the fiery death of Vern flashed.

Supper used his paw like a hand, his toenails like fingers, and clawed at his arm. More attention please. The dog had his eyes closed with his teeth half-bared in what passed for a smile.

At least someone was happy.

Wyatt stared out the window and watched the windmills turn lazily. He felt knotted up over what happened and had retreated to his room for the entirety of the day. He'd expected someone - his mother, Allie, maybe even Alexander - to come and talk to him. To discuss what had gone down.

But no one came. And he was getting the feeling that no one would ever come. That he could rot inside that room holding his own, private pity party while life went on as normal outside these four walls.

Hiding wasn't going to solve anything. He'd skipped breakfast and lunch. The call for dinner was almost an hour ago and Wyatt decided to see if there was anything left. He rolled off the bed and called Supper to follow.

———

The dining hall was mostly empty, as were the silver pans which typically held food. He passed by the scraps, instead snatching a pear from a bowl at the end of the line. It wasn't much, but as he bit down and juice filled his mouth, the taste made his stomach rumble. That reminded him of the presentation, and he muscled past the self-loathing and fled the room.

His plan to return to solitude was interrupted when he spotted Barbara, Allie, and Seth surrounding a roulette wheel and eating their own meals, all of which were more substantial than his pear. The only person he didn't know was the woman beside Seth, the one from the demonstration. Wyatt noticed that she had a few fingers entwined in his brother's hair and he suspected they were already more than friends.

He almost moved on, but Seth spotted him.

"Hey, brother."

Wyatt nodded. "I didn't think you associated with us commoners anymore." He tried to sound light, playful, but suspected the words came out with his true feelings instead.

Seth pretended not to notice. "You know how it is. Got to keep a pulse on things." He pointed to an empty chair. "Have a seat."

Wyatt did, sliding in beside Allie. She pointed to her plate. "We can share."

Wyatt shook his head. "Not much of an appetite. Not after..."

He hoped someone would take the hint.

Barbara was the first to speak. "That was unique."

Unique, Wyatt thought? We watched a boy get cooked alive. "Am I the only one that feels sick about that? I mean, the way people cheered. Like it was a goddamn show."

A heavier quiet fell over the table. Wyatt looked around at the faces. Allie had stopped eating and stared back at him with judging eyes.

"With what those cannibals did, killing our people." Barbara said. "He was executed for his crimes. And we know how brutal those monsters are. They eat other people, for crying out loud."

Wyatt noticed her change in tone, how she muttered the last part. How she said, 'our people'.

"Got what he deserved." Allie muttered in a low voice. "If we show weakness, that will be the end of us. All of us. You know that."

"Maybe." Wyatt said. He wished he could have pulled back on saying so much.

A long, uncomfortable silence passed before Barbara took mercy and ended it. "Seth, I didn't realize how much Papa trusted you. Some of the women say you're his understudy." Her voice was filled with pride, as if her son had just got an A plus on his spelling test rather than be the headliner in an execution.

Wyatt watched Seth beam with self-satisfaction. He was proud of himself too.

"Papa's amazing. He's taught me more about life, about myself, in the last few days than I ever thought possible. And he's shown me that I can be important. Not just the crippled kid no one wants to be around."

Rosario tousled his hair and he gave her hand a playful swat. "And he's been introducing me to everyone."

"Including your lovely, young lady friend." Barbara nodded to the woman beside him, who smiled back but didn't say anything.

"Oh, Wyatt." Seth turned to him. "You were late, and I just realized I haven't introduced you. Rosario, my brother Wyatt. Wyatt, Rosario."

Wyatt managed a smile. She looked a few years older, and much more experienced than Seth. The woman was almost model-beautiful, aside from vacant eyes. He wondered what she saw in his brother, then chided himself for being a jerk. Why shouldn't Seth be allowed a girlfriend?

He wanted to agree with their mother, to find some way to be happy that Seth was finding his way here. And probably getting laid by the looks of it. But it was hard to look at his brother and see the boy who he used to roll around with in the leaves. Now, all he could see was the guy who'd set fire to a defenseless kid.

Wyatt knew his mother and Allie were right. That everyone at the casino needed to be careful, to watch out for each other. But weren't there better ways to go about that?

Seth leaned into Rosario and his cheeks flared pink as he whispered something to her. She gave a wan smile and a nod. Then Seth turned to the others. "If you fine people will excuse us, Rosario and I have some pressing matters to attend to."

The woman took the handles of Seth's chair and turned him away from the table, and away from his family. As Wyatt watched them go, he realized Seth hadn't said a word about the execution or his part in it. It was as if a boy's death was as mundane as cleaning the carpets. Just another day on the job.

Wyatt pushed his chair away from the table and left without a word.

CHAPTER 23

WYATT STARTED AT THE NOTHINGNESS OF THE DESERT, LOST inside his head. He wondered what life was like beyond here, beyond the border. And he felt it calling him like a siren's son.

Would anyone even care if I left, he wondered. Seth had Papa. Their mother had her new beau Richard, who Wyatt knew made her happier than he'd seen her in years. Since before the bombs.

Allie might, but some words Pete had said to him months before stuck in his mind. *She'll take you for all she can get and spit you out like used gun when she gets bored.* Wyatt didn't exactly believe that, but he saw the way she flirted with Franklin and he suspected she'd move on soon enough if he took a hike.

He'd take Supper though. He knew that much. And the more he considered it, the notion of him and his dog wandering the world from one adventure to the next sounded pretty damn good. Especially in comparison to a place where they roasted boys like hogs at a 4th of July barbecue.

"We need to talk."

Wyatt turned to his mother, who stood a few yards behind him. The distance between them was only feet but felt like a chasm.

"Talk then," he said.

He knew that was rude and disrespectful. She was his mother, after all. But the woman who'd raised him wasn't the woman here now. That woman was kind and full of love. She wouldn't abide by what was happening here. He was unsure where this Barbara, hardened by the world, fit into his life now. Or him in hers.

"You're pulling away," Barbara said. "I can see it in your eyes.

There was no sense denying the truth so he waited for her to go on.

"You always were my gentle son, Wyatt. I loved that about you. And I know what happened at the demonstration bothered you." She took a step toward him, then another.

"I'd think it would bother anyone with a conscience," Wyatt said. "You know, I talked to that boy after we got back. His name was Vern. He was thirteen years old."

She remained silent, perhaps sensing he had more to say, and she was right. The more he talked the faster the words came.

"And you stood there, with everyone else, as they tortured him. Burned him alive. And then everyone fucking cheered like the Patriots had just won another goddamn Super Bowl! How is that right, mom?"

Barbara finished crossing the gap between them. They were close enough to touch but did not.

"I never said it was right, Wyatt. But that's the world we live in now."

He tilted his head back, unable to look at her. He stared at the gunmetal sky, trying to find something to focus on. A cloud. A bird. Anything. But it was a bleak and barren sea of emptiness.

"Do you remember the song I used to sing to you when you were little?" Barbara asked.

He could feel her body heat beside him but wouldn't look. He shook his head.

"It was from one a musical called *Betsy*. Your father took me to see it once at an off-Broadway revival, back when we were dating. I think the song's called *Blue Skies* but I'm not sure. I'd sing it to you when we were outside, especially on pretty days."

He felt her take his hand and give it a soft squeeze.

"Blue days, all of them gone. Nothing but blue skies, from now on," she sang, a little off-key. "Do you remember now?"

"A little," he lied.

"When I decided to leave Maine, I told you that I wanted to go because it wasn't safe. That I didn't want us to starve. But there was something I didn't tell you, I guess because it seemed so silly at the time. Especially after everything that had happened."

Wyatt finally looked at her and saw tears rolling from her remaining eye. He wiped them away with the backs of his fingers. "Tell me now."

"I wanted to see blue skies again."

He glanced at the sky which was anything but blue.

"It's a metaphor, Wyatt." She squeezed his hand harder. "Every day in Maine was sadder than the one before. Grayer than the one before. And I wanted--" She swallowed a sob. "I needed to go somewhere that there was hope. Not just for safety and food and warmth. But hope for better days."

She was full on crying now and the resentment he'd built up toward her melted away. He put his hands on his shoulders and pulled her into him. Her chest heaved against his.

"I feel like there's hope in this place. It's not perfect but there are good people here. A society. A plan for normalcy. And I want to be a part of that."

"Okay," Wyatt said. "Okay, mom."

He rubbed her back as she cried. He didn't share her optimism, but she was his mother and he owed it to her to try.

CHAPTER 24

SETH WAS IN LOVE. THE HEAD OVER HEELS VARIETY. HE HAD been since Papa introduced the two of them and, instead of her face clouding with disgust or pity, Rosario looked at him like a person. The time they spent in bed together soon after solidified the deal.

He loved everything about her. From her perfect body and the way she used it, to her gentle acceptance of his condition. She made it easy to be vulnerable in front of her. As much as he would have wanted things to be the other way around - him caring for her- he was learning to accept the situation.

As they made their way back to their room, passing by Papa's quarters, the man's voice called out. "Seth? Is that you?"

They turned to see the door ajar.

"Yeah. It's me and Rosie."

The electric whir of Papa's scooter approached and the door opened the rest of the way. "Why don't you join me for a minute?"

"Sure."

Rosario began to push Seth through the doorway but Papa held up his index finger.

"Ah, do you mind giving us a little privacy, hon? I'll have him back to you in one piece, don't worry." He gave her one of his patented comforting smiles and added a wink for good measure.

Rosario looked to Seth, as if he had authority over her.

"Go on to the room. I'll be over soon," Seth said.

She looked back and forth between the two men, finishing on Papa, then turned and left them. Seth wondered if there's been anything between the two of them. Papa had assured him that Rosario wasn't one his wives, but at random moments he picked up on a feeling, a vibe, that struck him odd. He kept that curiosity to himself. Maybe some things were better not known.

Papa stopped his chair at the dining room table where a glass of orange juice sat accompanied by a dinner plate. Seth wheeled himself over and saw Papa's dinner was far superior to what had been tendered in the dining hall. There was a medley of fresh vegetables, a fruit cup, and what looked like a steak. But that wasn't possible unless Papa and company had livestock hidden away somewhere.

Maybe he does, Seth thought. It wouldn't have surprised him considering all the other amenities at the casino. And it would only make sense that meat would be reserved for the leadership. For the important people. That was the way the world worked now.

Seth watched Papa slice through the meat on the plate. Not only watched but stared curious and envious. And Papa knew he was staring.

"An occasional treat," Papa said. "Most days I eat the same as the dishwashers and maids. But once in a great while I allow myself to be a glutton. All part of the sacrifice." He shoved a bit of the rare meat between his lips and chewed with his mouth open.

The smacking noises coupled with the occasional glimpse of masticated food and blood made Seth's own stomach heave and he looked away.

"It's an acquired taste, truth be told. I'd prefer a nice rump roast if I had my choice. Or maybe some venison. But from a young one though. Deer get gamey as they age. People aren't much different really."

Seth bobbed his head as it seemed the polite thing to do. Then his mind comprehended what Papa had actually said. "Wait. What?"

"I'm telling you about where this meat comes from, son."

Realization clanged in Seth's mind like a dull clash of thunder. No meat for anyone else... Sacrifices...

"Are you saying--"

"That is exactly what I'm saying." The words came out matter of fact, like he was teaching a child where that bacon came from pigs.

Seth made a weak attempt at concealing his disgust. His shock.

"Awe don't get your underwear in a bunch now. What should we have done? Thrown him out to be devoured by the bugs and vermin? You think Yahweh wants us to waste precious resources? No. He sends them to us so that we can thrive!"

"But the cannibals, they're our enemies. Aren't they?"

Papa blotted his mouth with a napkin and nodded. "But not because they're cannibals, son. Because they're Godless, murdering savages. Cannibalism is just a convenient buzz word. Gets those who aren't as enlightened as us riled up."

He cut off another chunk of man meat with disturbing eagerness and continued to eat. "To keep people under control, you must know what they fear. And if a boogeyman doesn't exist, we need to provide one. Otherwise..." He waved his fork through the air. "Anarchy."

Seth's head started to nod again even though he wasn't sure what his brain was doing.

"Yahweh provides for us. For our minds and for our bodies."

Us. Seth knew that us meant himself and Papa. Together.

"Though we are Yahweh's children like everyone else here, you and I are unique, Seth. And because of that He provides for our unique needs."

Papa put his utensils down and slid the plate across the table to Seth. The china made soft, protesting sounds as it glided over the Formica.

"Do you want to try some?" He asked, nonchalant.

"Uh, I... I ate a bunch at dinner. Stuffed, really." He patted his stomach, trying to infer that he would have gobbled it down if he still had an appetite, but the notion of it, despite Papa's assertions, was unbearable.

"Oh, come now. There's always room for dessert." He extended his fork to Seth, his smile now looking sinister rather than sincere.

Seth took the fork. He spun it between his fingers, procrastinating.

"When the Israelites were sent manna from Heaven, they didn't say, 'Thank you, maybe later.' They ate."

Seth gripped the fork and tried to shut down his mind. It was just meat, after all. Just meat. Not worth risking his relationship with Papa. His position in the community. Just meat.

He speared the smallest piece he could find. It was somewhere between the size of a nickel and a quarter. He could get that much down even if he had to swallow it whole.

"Eat, my son," Papa said. "Show Yahweh you appreciate His gifts. That you won't waste the sacrifice."

Seth shoved the morsel between his lips. Saliva flooded his mouth as the flavor overwhelmed his taste buds. It didn't taste like chicken. Or beef. Or pork. It was more like veal, but tougher, stringier. And by God, it was delicious.

"There ya go," Papa said.

Yes, he was doing it. He was proving himself to Papa. To Yahweh. To himself. There wasn't anything he couldn't do.

Until the memory of the boy's screams echoed through his head. He panicked and tried to swallow, tried to force the partially chewed food down his gullet, but everything else he'd eaten in the last hour was too busy making a hasty retreat.

Seth spun to the side, spotted a wastebasket within arm's reach and grabbed it just in time to--

Barf up the human meat, the fruit, the coffee, the potatoes he'd had for dinner. It all came out projectile style and the backsplash splattered against his face as he wretched into the can.

"That's okay," Papa said with a gentle chuckle. "You'll get used to it. Just remember, these nutrients sustain us and allows us to carry on Yahweh's mission here. We do this for Him."

Seth pulled at the sleeve of his shirt and wiped at his face as he nodded. He was relieved Papa wasn't angry with him for wasting the meat.

It will get easier with time, he told himself.

And then Papa will be pleased.

CHAPTER 25

NEXT TO RICHARD, THE BEST PART ABOUT LIFE AT THE CASINO was being able to go for a walk at night without worry. It was one of the simple pleasures that she'd so enjoyed in the days before the bombs. A glass of wine, a full belly, and a stroll through the dark, breathing in the cool, evening air.

She never thought she'd be able to do that again before ending up here. And even if her belly wasn't quite full, she wasn't about to let that ruin the moment.

A half dozen or so other members of the community wandered about, but the atmosphere was more relaxed during the night. Everyone seemed content to enjoy the relative solitude and quiet. No forced small talk. And she appreciated that. After the past few days, she needed to clear her head.

There were reminders that life wasn't normal. One of them was the guard who stood atop a wooden platform and surveyed the land around him. His desert fatigues stood out in stark contrast with the black night, but his presence was calming. Not normal, but safe.

The guard caught her staring and locked eyes with her. Embarrassed, she gave something between a wave and a salute. She was trying to be friendly but her awkward gesture made her feel self-conscious and she regretted it straight off.

She was surprised when the guard waved back. It wasn't what she was expecting, especially considering his position. She'd imagined these guards as similar to the unflappable, bearskin hat-wearing types who held station outside Buckingham Palace. Stone-faced and statuesque. Solemn and staid.

"You should have on a jacket," he called down to her.

Barbara shrugged. "I'm from Maine, remember? This is balmy compared to what I'm used to."

The guard flashed a broad grin. "If you say so. I've never been able to abide the cold. Especially out here in the desert. My crap luck I drew the short straw and got night watch."

"Want me to bring you some coffee?" Barbara asked.

The guard set aside the AK-47 which he cradled like a baby, bent down, then emerged with a thermos. "Already handled." He unscrewed the lid. "I'm Carlos."

"Barbara."

"Nice to meet you, Barbara."

He brought the thermos to his mouth again and tilted it back for a long drink. And then he froze.

Carlos' eyes stayed locked on her and grew wide, two cue balls against his tan face. At first, Barbara thought the coffee was too hot, that he'd scalded his mouth and didn't want to let on.

But then he dropped the thermos. He began to tilt forward, slow then picking up speed. His upper body broke the plane over the safety rail and the momentum he'd built up was too much, sending Carlos toppling over it, doing a single somersault as he fell from the platform.

His body slammed into the pavement, so close to Barbara that his hot blood splattered her face. She stared down in shock, trying to comprehend what just happened.

And then she saw what took his life. A thin, white spear jutted from his back.

A shrill whistling sound stole her attention away from Carlo's motionless body. Now she looked upward, toward the noise, and she saw what looked like flaming birds arcing through the black sky.

Before she could react to that, she heard glass breaking and fire erupted at dozens of spots around her, the flames licking the asphalt and setting ablaze anything within its orange grasp. The wooden platform upon which Carlos had been standing was hit with another Molotov cocktail and went up like a pyre.

We're under attack, she realized.

One after another the glass bombs rained over the fence. She heard a woman shriek and turned, finding the wretched sight of a girl sprinting as flames consumed her. The faster she ran the faster the fire spread and soon she was nothing more than a human-esque shape of fire and pain.

Barbara stepped towards her, knowing somewhere in her consciousness that she should help, but the burning woman was already too far gone. She collapsed, flailing and thrashing, screaming and bawling.

Before she could be the next person lit up, Barbara picked up her pace, scrambling for cover. Around her was more screaming, both in pain and panic, but intermixed with their cries she heard feet moving.

A glance backward, toward the desert, revealed wild men and women climbing over the fence. Breaching, and breaking, the safety the walls provided.

Twenty yards away a rifle went off. Ten shots, maybe fifteen. It was the other night guard. But any relief was short-lived when Barb saw a half-dozen cannibals scramble onto his platform and attack.

One of the savages cut his throat while another disemboweled him. Two of the cannibals grabbed hold of his spilled guts and gnawed away like it was rope sausage.

Barbara saw one of the attackers digging at Carlos' waist, then jerk his hand free with a fistful of keys. He raced to the main gate and worked at the lock.

I must get someone, Barbara thought. I must tell someone what's happening so they can stop this.

She turned, ready to sprint back to the casino but it was too late. Two of the invaders latched hold of her arms. She could feel their long, ragged fingernails digging into her flesh, then a pop, then warm blood oozing down her skin.

Barbara strained to break free, but the two captors were stronger, more desperate. Then she saw a third striding her way. It carried a white spear which now, closer, she realized was a femur. One end had been sharpened to a point, ready and able to impale her.

Her mind flashed back to the old house in Maine, the first time she experienced an attack like this. Except now her sons were nowhere around and Trooper was dead. This time she would lose more than an eye.

But the man ready to end her crumpled forward. His spear skittered across the pavement, stopping near her feet. She looked past it and found--

Richard's handsome face. It was dotted with black blood and she saw a spade shovel gripped in his hands. He swung the shovel, the blade colliding with the face of one of the cannibals who held her.

The metal hit just below the savage's cheek, cleaving his face in half as it shattered off his upper teeth which rained to the ground like ivory shrapnel.

Maybe shocked, maybe scared, the other cannibal who'd been holding Barbara let go and she didn't hesitate. She dropped to her knees, grabbed the spear, and spun around.

The femur sunk deep into the man's waist. His hands clawed at the bone, trying to free it from his abdomen, but Barbara gave it another push. He grunted out, "Bitch" as he tumbled sideways.

"If you wanted to get my attention, I can think of easier ways." Richard extended his hand and pulled her to her feet. Even with fires burning all around them and people screaming out, he could still crack jokes. It helped to calm her nerves, a little.

His calloused hand squeezed her arm, reassuring. He pushed her towards the casino, toward safety, but stopped. Barbara looked back at him. His mouth was open, but not to speak. Instead to unleash a torrent of blood.

A spear jutted from the back of his skull. His eyes met hers for a moment. Recognition flashed. Faded. Disappeared.

Barbara unleashed a scream as Richard fell, collapsing into her. She tried to hold him up, as if the act of keeping him on his feet would keep him alive, but he was too heavy, and his body slithered down hers before crumpling into the asphalt.

When she looked from the man she was falling in love with, the man she'd already thought of as her future, she found his killer. He wore a wild, bestial grin that revealed broken teeth. His tongue licked across them. Lustful. Hungry.

"You're uglier than my second wife," he said. "But she fucked like a wildcat. How 'bout you?"

Maybe it was the look on his face. Or the fact that her happiness and safety had once again been stolen. Or just because the bastard had called her ugly, but something inside snapped. Barbara dove at him and her sudden fury shocked the man so much he did nothing to stop her.

Her hands latched onto the cannibal's face. Her thumbs found his eyes. Barbara screamed as she pushed her digits into the sockets and no matter how much the man thrashed to shake her loose, she refused to let go.

The man's left eye popped out of his skull and dangled there like a yoyo at the end of the line. He grabbed it with his grimy fingers and tried to shove it back into the socket, but while he was distracted Barbara ripped the spear from the dead man's chest, spun around, and impaled the cannibal through the groin.

His dying howl was unlike anything she'd imagined and, as she watched blood gush from his pelvis, she couldn't suppress a manic cackle of glee.

Then, a new sound came into focus. Bullets firing in all directions. She looked back to the casino and found Alexander rushing toward her and shooting past her all at the same time. When he got to her side, he paused for barely a moment.

"You okay?"

She wasn't. But she nodded anyway.

He shoved her toward the building. "Get inside. I'll cover you."

That time, she listened.

CHAPTER 26

It seemed like fireworks exploding all around them. The climax as he thrusted on top of Allie felt dreamlike and somehow even better than the first time, they were together.

She'd come to him earlier that evening and, as was becoming their normal, they argued. Argued about the boy who's been executed so barbarically. Argued about Seth. Argued about Papa and the people at the casino. But the fire stoked by their back and forth raging turned into an inferno of passion.

It almost feels cliched, Wyatt thought as their sweat-slicked bodies clung to one another, their rapid heartbeats in sync. Like the couples in movies that fight then fuck. He'd always groaned when he saw that happen on screen. Turns out, real life was much better.

"Wow." Wyatt tried to catch his breath and say something more, but another loud bang ripped through the air and he realized it wasn't them after all; that was an actual explosion.

"What the hell?" Allie asked, raising her head off the pillow. He rolled off her, cool air replacing the space between them. In the moment they were silent, gunshots echoed outside.

Supper jumped to his feet beside the bed, barking.

Wyatt's nirvana-like ecstasy vanished as he realized what was happening. "It's an attack!" A chorus of screams confirmed his assessment.

"Attacked?" Allie parroted, but Wyatt didn't hear her as he yanked his jeans up and zipped them. He reached for his shirt which was in a pile with Allie's clothes.

"What are you doing?" She slipped her naked body free of the covers.

"I'm going to help."

"Please don't, Wyatt. You can't leave!"

Wyatt ignored her protests, turning his attention to the dog. "Supper, you stay and protect her."

Supper bounced onto the bed, planting himself between the two humans as Wyatt opened the hotel room door. He checked the hall in both directions. Empty.

"Wyatt don't go out there. You don't even got a gun! Wyatt looked back at her and put a finger to his lips. "Lock the door behind me."

He moved into the hall, easing the door closed in a barely audible click, then moved toward the source of the violence.

Through windows he saw fires raging outside, people running. Some were desperate and panicked. Some calculated and fighting. Muffled screams and shouts and explosions seeped into the building.

As he slipped through an exit, Wyatt strained to listen for voices he recognized, but then he saw the carnage. The bodies of the people he had met not long ago were on the ground, their faces now vacant and gray and bloody.

There were other bodies too, skinny, dirty corpses with tattered clothing. Cannibals. He saw a spear honed from human bone lying beside one of them and grabbed it as he passed by.

A scream came from close by, but just out of view. Wyatt turned and followed the direction of the sound and it was only a dozen paces before he spotted two cannibals. They loomed over someone on the ground, attacking.

"Hey!" Wyatt gripped the spear, readying himself.

The cannibals spun his direction and galloped at him, wild and frantic. The taller of the two, a man who looked like Frankenstein with anorexia, clutched a hatchet. His long strides helped him reach Wyatt first and he swung the weapon sidearm in a wide arc.

Wyatt dropped to his knees to avoid having his head taken off. As the hatchet sliced through the air above him, he rammed the spear into the tall cannibal's frail chest, burying it between rows of ribs. The man took two staggering steps backward, taking the spear with him and leaving Wyatt unarmed.

Which wasn't good because the second wild man, a red-haired bastard with a braided beard that hung halfway to his concave stomach, was on him. The man tackled Wyatt like a linebacker, and both hit the ground in a rolling, flailing heap.

The stink of the man, a sour mixture of rot and B.O. from hell, was enough to make Wyatt's guts contract as he fought to keep down his dinner. But he had the advantage because he was well-fed and strong.

The cannibal felt light as a sack of flour as Wyatt hurled him to the side where he crashed into a ceramic planter which housed a cactus. The pot fell over and onto the cannibal who wailed as scores of needles punctured his skin.

Wyatt glanced sideways where the tall cannibal remained upright but was beyond fighting. The man had dropped his hatchet in a vain attempt to use his hands to try to pull the spear from his chest and Wyatt lunged for it.

He grabbed the weapon and turned back to the smaller cannibal who was preoccupied with plucking the barbs from his face and neck. He didn't even notice Wyatt coming until the hatchet was already embedded in his skull.

Wyatt jerked it free and the man fell to the ground where he bled out. Then he continued toward the lifeless lump of a person who the two cannibals had been mauling before his arrival. Even though she was face down he recognized the white coat, the majority of which was now deep crimson with blood. To be sure she was gone, he rolled her onto her back.

It was Ramona Sidaris, the doctor who had given him the tetanus shot. A ragged bite had been taken out of her face. Another had excised a chunk of flesh from her neck. She was gone.

He almost left her but noticed the keyring on her belt. He knew all the community's medical supplies were locked up and couldn't risk letting those be stolen, so he pulled off the keys and dropped them into his pocket before moving on.

When he reached the front gates, Wyatt realized how unprepared the community was for this attack. Alexander's group of protectors seemed to have control of the situation now, but the body count belied the horror of what came before their arrival.

The corpses of dozens of men and women littered the ground. Some had been hacked to pieces. Some burned and smoldered. And some, although not enough, where cannibals who bled from gunshot wounds.

In his peripheral vision he saw his mother running inside the main entrance, then he found Alexander a few yards away, rifle at his shoulder, ensuring none of the savages got close.

He breathed a little easier seeing that his mother was safe, but his mind immediately shifted to Seth. He had no way of knowing if any cannibals had breached the casino, but he had to find out. Despite his revulsion over Seth setting the boy on fire, Wyatt wasn't going to let anything happen to his brother. He wasn't going to lose another member of his family.

CHAPTER 27

Rosario gripped Seth's shoulder so tight it hurt. He wanted to shake it away, but felt he had to accept the pain. To be brave. To *be a man*, as the saying went.

But he wasn't a man. He was sixteen years old and so scared he had to keep a vise grip on his asshole to keep from shitting his pants.

He could feel the woman, his woman, trembling, and tried to think of words to placate her. To alleviate her fear. "We'll be fine," he said. "The protectors will never let them into the casino."

That was little solace, even if true, because people were being slaughtered outside. Many, from the sound of it. The screams serenaded them like music from a Puccini opera and Seth had a sickening feeling this was a losing battle.

It's not supposed to be like this, Seth thought. Papa promised safety and we did everything God wanted, so why was this happening? Could this really be part of some grander plan?

Before he could put too much thought into it there was a bang against their hotel room door. A gasping voice followed. "Seth!"

"Was that Papa?" He asked Rosario.

She stared at the door with wide, fear-filled eyes, still not releasing him. "I don't know."

Seth couldn't take any chances. If Papa needed him, it was his duty to come. Because even if Papa believed Seth would be the man to lead this community, he wasn't ready yet. There was too much to do. Too much to learn.

He slipped free of Rosario's grasp and wheeled himself to the door. When he reached to unlock it, his hand trembled and he focused, trying to steady himself, to not let his beautiful, perfect girl-friend see his weakness.

He opened the door and pushed himself halfway into the hall. It was empty. And silent.

"Close the door! Now!" Rosario said, the fear in her voice escalating.

He turned to her and smiled. "We're fine. No one's there."

As soon as the last word left his mouth, Seth was pulled out of the room. A deranged face stared down at him. The mouth was contorted into a gleeful leer. Like a man who'd just been delivered the world's tastiest steak.

"Lock the door, Rosario!" Seth yelled as he clawed at the man's face. Under his fingers he could feel slick blood, dirt, and grease.

The man cannibal swiped at him with a large dagger. Seth leaned sideways just in time to dodge the blade which plunged through the leather wheelchair seat. Where his non-existent leg would have been.

For the first time since being maimed, Seth was grateful for having only one leg.

As the cannibal jerked the dagger free, a shower of shattered ceramic cascaded over the both of them. The man went limp, falling face first into Seth's lap, unconscious.

Seth looked over this shoulder and found Rosario holding the remnants of a destroyed lamp. "Thank you," he said.

She flashed a nervous, but still stunning smile. "Any time."

Seth grabbed fistfuls of the cannibal's filthy, matted hair and pushed him away. He landed on the floor with a heavy thud. He was eager to return to the safety of the room, but Rosario stepped past him, toward the cannibal.

"I think he's out," Seth said.

Rosario nodded. "He is. But he's still alive." She reached into her back pocket and pulled out a folding hunting knife.

"Rosie, you don't--"

She didn't wait for him to finish, instead flicking the knife open and crouching over the fallen cannibal. His dazed eyes stared up at her, unseeing, as she slammed the blade into his throat. A small fountain of blood shot up and out of the wound and the man seemed to come around at the worst possible time - for him.

As she stabbed him again and again and again Seth's gaze shifted back and forth between his girlfriend to the dying man whose arms and legs twitched in helpless horror. He was shocked but impressed. And he realized that Papa hadn't just brought the two of them together solely because she was beautiful, but because she was powerful and relentless. His own sexy bodyguard. He felt himself getting hard and shifted in his seat to hide it.

When Rosario stopped stabbing the man, she looked back at Seth with a blood-splattered face and blazing eyes. Seth wasn't sure whether he should thank her or drag her into the bedroom for a frantic fuck but before he could make up his mind, pounding footsteps stole his attention.

He braced himself, turning toward the noise, and saw his brother sprinting up the hall. Seth wanted to tell him he was too late, that Wyatt didn't need to ride to the rescue this time.

Then he heard Papa bellow in pain.

CHAPTER 28

WYATT GLANCED AT THE DEAD CANNIBAL ON THE FLOOR. IT looked as if the entirety of the man's blood had drained into the carpet, painting a scarlet pattern through the fiber. All he cared about was that the man was dead.

Once that was confirmed he grabbed onto the handles of Seth's wheelchair and shoved him toward his room, ignoring Seth's pleas to stop.

"We have to help Papa." Seth tried to stop the wheels from moving but Wyatt didn't pause, not caring if he broke his brother's fingers in the process.

"I will. You're staying in your room." He knew Seth would hate him for this. For treating him like a child. Like an invalid. But that didn't matter if he stayed alive.

"Stop it," Seth said as he thrashed in the chair.

Wyatt had him through the doorway and gave another hard shove that sent him five feet inside the room. Then he turned to Rosario. "If you let him out of here and anything happens, I'll kill you."

The woman nodded. Maybe Seth didn't grasp the seriousness of the situation, but she did.

Seth had already spun his chair toward the door. "Fuck your hero shit, Wyatt, I'm--"

Wyatt backed out of the room and slammed the door. He heard it lock and breathed a bit easier as he moved one room up, where Papa's door hung ajar.

Fearing a trap, Wyatt peeked into the darkened space. He strained, trying to discern whether someone waited behind the door. Waited to attack.

All he could hear were grunts and groans and occasional chatter deeper inside. He squeezed his palm around the handle of the hatchet and slipped through the opening.

There was no trap. But there was certain and immediate danger. Papa's guards, the braindead bruiser twins, laid dead on the linoleum. One had been stabbed to the death. The other has his head caved in. Despite Wyatt's misgivings toward the men, they didn't deserve that.

As he stepped over their bodies, he spotted Papa sprawled on the floor beside his couch. A cannibal straddled his mountain-like midsection, a sight that made Wyatt think of riding an old horse. The savage had a knife pressed into Papa's bare chest, drawing thin, white lines in abstract loops and swirls.

The glass coffee table was shattered, the floor covered with the exploded shards. As Papa struggled some of them sliced into his back fat and rivulets of blood leaked out.

"Fat piggy's gonna be good eatin'!" A bald man said, and Wyatt realized there were three cannibals in the room. The one mounting Papa, the bald man, and a woman whose dust-brown hair was so wild she could have been an extra in a movie set in prehistoric times.

"I'm gonna fry up his big ole belly like bacon!" The rider said, his words peeling off into laughter. "Finger lickin good!"

"That was chicken," baldy said.

"You two shut your mouths already. I get first dibs. That fucker killed my boy!' The woman bounced on her feet as she spoke. In each hand she held knives. "I'm gonna roast his cock like a hot dog and gobble it down!"

The men looked to each other, exchanging an uncomfortable sneer at the thought of cock-gobbling.

Three against one. Wyatt didn't like those odds, not one bit. But he knew going back for help would take too long. And as much as he hated Papa for the horrific demonstration, he now understood the enemy they were up against.

He wasn't going to let these monsters win.

On a nearby end table he saw a candle in a glass jar. He grabbed it and estimated it weighed a pound or more. It might work if his aim was good.

And it was.

The jar slammed into the skull of the cannibal who had turned Papa into his own, personal pack mule. It made a dull crunch and Wyatt wasn't sure whether that was the jar breaking or the savage's cranium. He supposed it didn't matter. The man toppled sideways, bouncing off the couch before hitting the floor.

The other two cannibals shifted their attention to Wyatt and the bald man came first. He bounded over his fallen comrade, barreling forward, but Wyatt was ready.

He reared back with the hatchet and swung, planting the blade into the center of the cannibal's chest. The man's eyes grew so wide Wyatt wouldn't have been shocked to see them fall from his face as he fell into him.

The impact sent Wyatt backward and off-balance. He stumbled into the wall and shook the man off him but now the feral woman was on him and his hatchet was still embedded in the dying man's sternum.

"You fuckers think you scare us?" She screamed as she stabbed with one of the knives. The blade slashed through Wyatt's upper arm creating a shockwave of pain. "Torch my boy to send us a message? We'll eat every last one of you to the bone!"

She lashed out with the other knife. That one caught Wyatt in the side and he felt the blade ricochet off his ribs.

He latched hold of her hair with both hands, craning her neck as far back as his arms could push. Breaking someone's neck always looked so easy in the movies. Real life was harder.

She squawked, arms flailing, each gesture sending steel blades in Wyatt's direction, but she couldn't see to aim and none of these new blows landed.

Wyatt pushed harder, jerking her head side to side. Maybe he couldn't snap her neck like a dry twig, but a concussion could buy him time.

The woman made another flailing attempt with the knife and that one landed. It plunged deep into Wyatt's forearm and he lost his grip with that hand. He strained to keep her at arm's length, to contain her ferocious fury, but he was losing.

He had a moment to think about his family. About Supper. He wondered if they'd be okay if this wild woman ended him.

And then he saw a hand reach around the woman's throat. A hand holding a jagged eight-inch long shard of glass.

Wyatt's eyes adjusted and he saw Papa standing behind the cannibal just as the big man sliced open her neck from one side to the other.

She turned her head to see who had cut her and in doing so the wound gaped open wide enough to expose tendons and muscle, veins and arteries. To Wyatt it was like an up close and personal anatomy lesson.

The woman fell to the floor and bled out on the white carpet. Carpet Wyatt thought would never come clean again. Then he looked up and saw Papa grinning.

"We make a good team, my child." He dropped the shard of glass.

Wyatt scanned the room, double and triple-checking to make sure there were no other cannibals, no more danger. But they were alone.

They had survived.

CHAPTER 29

"This isn't easy work, not for any of us. But we all know why it's necessary." Papa spoke out over the crowd, which was now much smaller than before. "No one signs up for this voluntarily."

The survivors looked like refugees. Their faces masks of dejection and fear. There were no Amens, no shouts of agreement or encouragement. The only sound that broke the silence was weeping.

Wyatt couldn't help but compare it to the demonstration when the bustling crowd was bloodthirsty and cocky as they celebrated death. Now that death had come to them, their attitudes had changed, and he wondered if it all could have been prevented. He wondered why it had to come to this.

His bandaged arm was around his mother whose body shook with sobs. He squeezed her shoulder, trying to give comfort. At his other side Allie looked to Papa. She wasn't distraught, but the fearful, worried expression he'd seen so often on her face during their time on the road was back and worse than ever before.

Allie reached over and grabbed his free hand, squeezing it. His skin was ripped and blistered from digging graves all night long, but her touch still felt comforting. More comforting than Papa's words, that sounded hollower to his ears than ever before.

"Our fallen men and women are heroes of the highest order and right now they're dining at Yahweh's table. They are feasting in ways you and I can only dream. But one day, my children, we'll be with them again. We'll all be together, victorious and rewarded in Heaven."

As Wyatt gazed across the crowd, he thought the group looked broken physically as well as spiritually. The sight of many of them clad in black suits and dresses, formal wear which was common in the world before, looked bizarre and anachronistic in this wasteland where ripples of smoke still rose from the ground and the stench of burning bodies and death filled the air. They could have been stock-brokers or bankers, but their battered and bandaged faces belied the reality.

These people were losers. They'd lived with their heads in the clouds, promised safety by a morbidly obese motivational speaker who was talking out of his ass. When Hell came to them, they folded like a tower of cards. The only miracle to be found was that any of them were still alive.

Wyatt looked to the protectors. Their desert camo uniforms were blood-stained, and their faces carried the shame of a battle poorly fought. By his count, five of them had died the night before leaving only seven, counting Alexander.

The man Wyatt had viewed as a comic book hero upon their first meeting looked like a defeated soldier at the end of a deleterious battle. His eyes, once so fierce and eager, seemed dull as old marbles and, when Alexander realized he was being watched, he let his gaze fall to the ground.

Wyatt pitied him but was also angry. His mother had told him there were only two guards on duty at the time of the attack. How could these people have a virtual fortress yet live so unprepared? The more he thought about it, the more his rage built.

"We've made sacrifices to build this place, to make it into our own paradise, even though I'm sure for many of you, right now, it feels more like hell." Papa stood in front of the crowd, on one side of the graves, while everyone else was on the other. Even now he was still separated from the rest of the community, and with more guards surrounding him like spokes on a wheel, each keeping a careful eye to any threats.

"We know that more today than ever before..." Papa took out a handkerchief and blotted his face, wiping away sweat. "This life, the righteous one. Living for Yahweh has its own trials and tribulations. But it has its rewards. And for that, we are forever grateful." His voice broke on the last words, overcome with a choking, coughing fit.

"Love you, Papa." Someone said from the front of the crowd.

Papa's eyes filled with tears. He covered his mouth with the handkerchief while he cleared his throat of phlegm and seemed to regain his composure as he looked up at the person who spoke.

"Thank you, my child." Then he turned to the crowd, but Wyatt thought he looked unsteady on his feet. He wondered how much longer the man would be able to stand. "We must accept that our path to glory will be littered with trials and tribulations. And this," he gestured out to the graves. "This is one of them. And let me promise you, vengeance will be ours."

There was a long pause, as if Papa was waiting for praise that didn't come. Then--

"Why did this happen, Papa?" A man in a suit asked. "We've lost so many..."

Papa straightened his back, steeling himself. "We could not foresee last night's violence, but Yahweh did. That's why he brought our new friends to the community. Because, my children, without our friend Wyatt I'd be in one of these graves." He stomped his foot on the ground for effect. "I would be dead were it not for him."

Everyone, even Allie and Barbara who were right beside him, turned to look at Wyatt, whose eyes widened in surprise. He didn't expect to be recognized today, of all days, and especially not by Papa.

"Bless you, Wyatt." Myrtle said. Other, grateful voices followed.

The survivors moved to him, patting his shoulder, shaking his hand. He felt like a political candidate at a campaign rally and was uncomfortable with the attention.

"Wyatt, my deepest, most sincere gratitude. Thank you." Papa said. "I don't think I said that to you last night, but let me say it now, in front of everyone. I owe you my life."

Allie rubbed his back. Her hand slid down, first cupping his ass then giving it a squeeze. Wyatt felt his face and skin burning.

Missing from the adulation, was any reaction from Barbara. Her eyes were vacant and haunted and locked on Richard's freshly dug grave as she cried silent tears. He wondered how many more deaths the woman could bear. First her husband. Then Trooper. Now Richard. Was there a limit on how many loved ones a person could lose before they were irreparably broken?

He supposed that was a question for God. Or, as Papa would say, Yahweh. In the meantime, all Wyatt could do was pray that this be the last life she had to mourn.

He had no idea how soon that prayer would be denied.

CHAPTER 30

As the crowd dispersed Wyatt waved at Seth to join them. Throughout the funerals, his brother had sat beside Rosario and Franklin, never meeting his gaze. But now, with fewer faces in the crowd, it was impossible to ignore him.

Seth gave a curt nod, then leaned toward Rosario who'd been pushing his chair. He said something to her, then took hold of his own wheels and changed course, moving toward his family while Rosie followed the others into the casino.

"Hey," Wyatt said, unsure why things had to be so awkward. They were family, after all. Hell, he'd cleaned Seth's shitty ass more times than he could count. Besides, he hadn't done anything wrong.

Seth looked to Barbara, reaching out and taking her hand. "How are you holding up?"

Barbara peeled her eyes from Richard's burial plot and looked to her youngest son. "What?"

She reminded Wyatt of a cracked windshield, covered with spiderwebs of cracks and ready to shatter at any given moment.

"I asked how you are." Seth rubbed his thumb across the back of her hand, consoling.

"Oh. I'm... here." She tried to smile. Failed.

Seth looked sideways at Wyatt, his expression going cold. "Maybe I should ask for your autograph. Since you're such the fucking celebrity now."

"I didn't ask for any of that," Wyatt said.

"But you found it anyway. Always the golden boy. Rising to the occasion while I'm locked away like your dirty secret."

Wyatt rocked back and forth on his feet. He didn't want to fight, especially now, here, in front of their mother. Why couldn't Seth see how fragile she was? "Come on, brother. It was crazy last night. I just didn't want anything to happen to you."

"Really? Because it didn't seem like that to me."

Wyatt opened his mouth to respond but Alexander sidled up next to them. The man rested his hand on Barbara's forearm. "Let me just tell you how sorry I am about Richard. He was one of our best. And he wasn't shy about letting everyone know how special he thought you were."

Barbara's lip quivered and she made no attempt to speak.

"I'm sorry I didn't get there in time to help you both," Alexander said.

Barbara swiped at the tears rolling down her cheeks, but it was a losing battle. "You do not have to be sorry for anything," she said. "There's a reason for everything. Isn't that what they say?"

Alexander shrugged his shoulders. "Some do, I guess."

Barbara's facade broke and her quiet cries turned into wracking sobs. Wyatt reached for her, but Allie stepped between them. "Come inside, Barb," she said. "Let's get you washed up and something to drink."

She steered her away and Wyatt supposed that might be for the best. Men didn't know how to deal with a crying woman, himself included. And Allie has experienced her own losses, so she might be the best person to handle his mother in her fragile state.

He watched them disappear into the casino, then looked back to Seth and Alexander, but Seth was gone too. Wyatt followed the tracks his wheels had left in the dirt and saw him moving toward one of the casino's side entrances.

He shook his head, wondering how long and intensive the process of rebuilding that fence would be, then turned his attention to Alexander, looking like a shadow of the man he'd been days earlier. Gone was the confidence that set him apart from everyone else. He was less a superman, now just a man.

"I'm assembling a team. Can I count on you?" Alexander said.

"For what?" But he knew the reason.

"Come on, Wyatt." Alexander scowled. "We're not letting this go by without retaliation."

Wyatt understood this was coming. He'd felt the gravitas of the situation with every shovelful of dirt. "When?"

"Three hours."

Wyatt's eyes grew wide. "Are you kidding? That's not enough time to plan any--"

Alexander leaned in close enough for Wyatt to smell his sweat. "We don't need a plan. This isn't a mission. It's an extermination." He looked Wyatt up and down, examining. "Meet us in the armory in half an hour."

Alexander turned and left Wyatt alone, trying to figure out how he was going to tell his mother and Allie the plan.

CHAPTER 31

"What do you mean you're going out there again?" Allie paced back and forth, hands flailing. "Are you insane?"

Wyatt reached for her hand, but she pulled it away before he could catch her. He knew she needed time, time he didn't have. He looked to his mother who sat on the bed. Supper laid across her lap but all she seemed to care about was nursing the glass of booze she held in her hand like it was liquid gold.

"Alexander wants to end this once and for all," Wyatt said.

"So, let him. Tell him to take his 'roid raging buddies out there and go all Wild West on the cannibals. But don't go with them."

"What difference does it make?" Barbara said, words slurred. "It's not like it's any safer here."

Allie and Wyatt both looked to her, then each other. Wyatt wanted to grab her, to kiss her, to tell her how much he loved her, but his mother's presence made that awkward and impossible.

"Allie, they expect me to help. I can't hide. If you want to stay here, I have to do this."

"Don't make this about me. I don't want this. Not you going out there the day after those monsters killed dozens of us."

"It's the cost of living in a community," Wyatt said. "I don't get a free ride."

"You saved Papa's fat ass. That should count for something."

Wyatt checked the clock on the wall. He was running out of time and this was going nowhere.

"I'm sure it'll be okay. Alexander and the protectors know what they're doing," Wyatt said.

"Do they? Because the way I see it, this is just taking you down a path that will never end."

"It'll end when all those fucking cannibals are dead," Barbara pushed Supper off her lap and stood up. She wasn't as far in the bag as Wyatt had thought and there was more life in her eyes than he'd seen all day. "It's either that, or we all end up burned and eaten."

"So, you want your son to go out there and risk his life?" Allie asked.

Barbara glared at her. "You think we should just let them get away with what they did? Let them live after they killed Richard?" She swallowed a sob. "And the others," she said in an afterthought.

Wyatt felt sick over the pain and hate in her voice. He wanted no part of a search and destroy mission in the desert but if it was between that and being here, caught up in a feud between the two women in his life, he'd take the mission.

"I have to go." He gave his mother a quick peck on the cheek. Allie a longer kiss on the lips. Supper a thorough belly rub. And then he was gone.

CHAPTER 32

THERE WERE FOURTEEN OF THEM IN ALL. SEVEN PROTECTORS, six volunteers, and himself. The pace was triple what they'd used on the supply run. A steady, draining jog with only short reprieves to eat and shit, and then continue on.

They'd been at it for two and a half days now and the incessant march was a good excuse for Wyatt to keep quiet. While the others chattered about what they were going to do to the cannibals, Wyatt wanted no part in their grim fantasies.

Some of the protectors declared they'd rape the cannibal women while the males watched. Others wanted to sever limbs while they were still alive, saving the head for last. Clark's grand plan involved something he called *The Wasting* and, so far as Wyatt could gather, it involved shoving knives into the cannibals' spinal cords to paralyze them, then letting them starve to death.

Their bloodlust didn't surprise Wyatt. He knew certain people reacted this way to being attacked. He understood that violence begat violence. But the ferocious glee on their faces as they discussed how they would dole out pain and death made him realize he'd never be a part of their cadre, nor did he want to be.

"Penny for your thoughts?"

Wyatt was so lost in his thoughts that he hadn't realized Alexander was beside him. Until now, Alexander had kept his distance, possibly sensing that Wyatt wanted - needed - to be left alone.

Even now Wyatt was unsure whether he wanted to reconnect with the man he'd thought of as a friend. Because, while Alexander hadn't conjured up any gruesome revenge ideas of his own, he was still the leader of this group and he did nothing to quell the talk. Permission by silence.

Wyatt hesitated, choosing his words deliberately. "This makes me uncomfortable."

Alexander raised a dusty eyebrow. "The mission?"

"Yes." Wyatt slowed his pace to slip back from the rest of the group and fall out of earshot. "You saved us and brought us into the community. And I appreciate that, Alexander. I do. The thought of a new home, a new start, after all those terrible months on the road, it was more than I ever dreamed possible. And then you made it even better and promised us safety."

"You're saying I oversold it?"

"No. Not exactly. But I'm tired of the violence. Of the death."

Alexander nodded. "That's why we're going to finish it. So, we can live in peace once and for all."

"Do you really believe that? You don't think some other group's going to wander in and try to take what's ours and start this fighting all over again? Because I think you're smarter than that." Wyatt worried that might have been too far but getting the thoughts out of his head and into the open was freeing.

Alexander waited a good half minute before responding. "I'm starting to worry about you, Wyatt." Alexander said finally. "I know you'll have our backs when the time comes, but this talk is concerning. You can't have any doubts."

Wyatt looked ahead at the others. Raucous laughter emanated from the group, a joke neither of them had heard. One the men turned, as if wanting Alexander to join in the revelry, but when he saw that Alexander was in a private conversation with Wyatt, he turned back around. As much as Wyatt would have wanted to go back to the casino and be with his family, to go to his hotel room and hold Allie in bed with Supper at their feet, Alexander was right.

He was part of this now whether he wanted to be or not. The time to turn back had expired a long time ago. He needed to stay focused on the task at hand.

"You don't have to worry, I'm alright. I just miss Supper."

To Wyatt's relief, Alexander laughed at the double meaning in his joke.

Clark dropped back to meet them on the path. He made a chopping gesture with his hand. "I think we're getting close, boys. I can smell their stink every time the wind blows."

Wyatt thought he was crazy but sniffed the air anyway. His nose provided no vital information and he assumed, as usual, Clark was full of shit.

The group ahead had stopped in the shade of a low mesa and went to work on their supplies and rations. Alexander grabbed a pair of binoculars from his pack and raised them to his face, scanning the vast nothingness ahead.

Wyatt tried to follow his gaze, looking far ahead and sending his up-close vision out of focus. That was why he couldn't make sense of the white thing that flew past his face. Until he heard the whooshing sound.

The noise transported Wyatt back to the first battle. And he knew.

He turned to Alexander, ready to tell him to duck, that they were under attack. He saw Alexander's eyes wide with shock and he realized the binoculars were gone. Wyatt glanced down and saw them on the ground. Alexander's hands still held them.

Still Wyatt struggled to connect the dots until he returned his attention to Alexander and saw his forearms had been transformed into two blunted, bleeding stumps.

CHAPTER 33

"Fucking shit!" Clark screamed as he dove face first into the dirt.

The others panicked. Some sought cover behind assorted rocks or bushes while others followed Clark's lead and flattened themselves on the ground to lessen their target.

Wyatt saw an axe laying in the dirt past them and realized it was the object that had robbed Alexander of his hands. Then he heard another woosh. This time he was smart enough to drop.

The incoming spear caught Alexander in his shoulder, spinning him around just in time for--

Another spear to catch him in the chest. They stuck out at opposing angles and, when Alexander fell, the weapons held him partially upright. Blood drained from his mouth as did the life from his eyes.

Bullets whizzed past Wyatt's head. For a moment he didn't know where they came from until his head cleared and he heard the signature reports of the AKs. The protectors fired in every direction. Left, right. Front, back. Wyatt thought they were going to cut each other to pieces before the cannibals could even finish them off if they weren't careful.

But caution was gone. This was pure, wild panic and nothing more.

More spears soared toward them. A man named Javier who Wyatt only remembered because of the way the man had sucked on his teeth as he discussed how he was going to rape the cannibal's women - or as he called them, squaws - was impaled through the face. His head looked like a tomato on a shish kebab as he spun, hands gripping the weapon and trying to pull it free.

Wyatt made the mistake of thinking it couldn't get worse. Because then it got much worse.

Spears and axes and hatchets and arrows rained down, a hurricane of incoming hell. He saw arms cut off, torsos explode, arrows take out eyes. One of the female protectors caught an axe with her midsection and the force sliced her nearly in half.

The gunfire slowed from a steady chorus to the occasional report. Wyatt tried to see who was still alive and shooting but the second he raised his head an arrow zipped by, missing him by a few inches.

Through the screams and moans he heard a lone voice. Clark's. "Go! Behind that rock formation!" Clark pointed at a four feet high, amber-colored boulder that sat a few yards away.

Wyatt thought the distance too far, a suicide run, but Clark held up his rifle and Wyatt knew what he meant. *I'll cover you.*

Clark's rifle erupted.

Wyatt jumped to his feet and loped forward in a bent over gallop. He saw cannibals rushing toward them, not a few. Dozens. The whooped and yelped in triumphant glee.

How were we so stupid, Wyatt thought? We never had a chance.

One cannibal pulled out a knife and ripped it across Alexander's throat. He gave a second hack and then Wyatt watched his friend's head tumble to the ground with a thud. The cannibal kicked it like a midfielder passing to the striker and the receiving savage booted it forward.

This was what had become of the man who'd saved Wyatt and his family. The man he longed to impress. Who he thought of as something akin to big brother.

But now wasn't the time to mourn. It was the time to run.

CHAPTER 34

THE BULLETS STOPPED AND WYATT RISKED A GLANCE BACK AT Clark who was shoving another magazine into his rife. A female cannibal who was naked from the waist up sprinted at him, a knife in her hand.

Wyatt opened his mouth to scream, to warn him, but no words came out. He tried again. Nothing. It was like God had hit the mute button on his voice and he couldn't switch it back on.

Then he felt the pain in his belly. He looked down and saw a spear, no bigger around than a garden hose, protruding from his waist. He grabbed onto it ready to pull it free then felt the fire in his back.

A glance over his shoulder proved what he'd been reluctant to accept. He's been impaled.

Then hands were on him. He thought they belonged to a cannibal and raised his fist, not that he had the strength to fight back, but it was Clark.

Clark grabbed hold of the spear and in one swift motion jerked it free. Wyatt felt like his head was going to float off his body, like his bones had been replaced with jelly.

"Run you dumb motherfucker!"

Wyatt turned around now, holding a hand over his stomach, blood seeping through his fingers. He tried to run but felt like he had fifty-pound weights around his ankles. Every step was like running a mile.

"Keep going!" Clark yelled at his back, pushing him. He tried to pick up speed, this time making a left at the rock formation and drifting off the path. Somewhere ahead of him he heard water flowing, fast. A warm trickle of blood started running down his leg. He looked down and saw it soaked through his jeans. Too much blood. Soon he wouldn't be able to run anymore.

When they reached the creek, Wyatt looked past Clark and toward the mob of rushing cannibals. They looked like a stampede of stick figures; their tanned skin stretched taut over their bones. And then, all at once, they stopped running.

Clark pushed Wyatt into the water. He lost his balance on slick rocks and fell hard, cracking his head and the world blinked black.

When his sight back he saw the cannibals had pulled out bows and arrows. All drawn and ready to fire. He wanted to tell Clark to duck.

But it was too late.

Clark was hit in the neck and tumbled sideways, face first into the muddy water. Blood mingled with the silt, turning the area around them deep crimson.

Wyatt felt an arrow hit him in the upper arm, but it was a superficial wound and went straight through. Another soared just by his face and splashed into the creek.

The next arrow hit Wyatt in the chest. He looked down at it, puzzled by this new addition to his torso. Blood spurted from the wound. He grabbed it, but between his diminished strength and the slick blood he couldn't get a grip.

Then an arrow caught him in the side. And another landed in his chest, just inches away from the first.

Everything seemed to slow down. His body felt cold, not from the creek, but from the inside out. He thought he should be in pain, but he was numb. And for some reason, that was okay.

Wyatt slumped back in the water, felt it wash over him. He let his head dip into the stream. His ears filled, sounding like the ocean in conch shells. It trickled across his face. Into his mouth. It tasted sweet and he swallowed it down.

His eyes fluttered, closed.

And he felt a euphoric peace fill him up from the tip of his toes to the top of his head.

Somewhere inside he realized this was wrong. He needed to get up, but all he could do was let the water cradle and carry him away. He needed to get back to his family and tell them what was in his heart. He had the words now. He needed his mother and Allie to know everything was going to be alright. He had to tell Seth to take care of Supper.

But the comforting creek was too seductive to leave.

He couldn't hear the screams or the yells. He felt no pain. He wasn't scared anymore.

And everything faded away.

CHAPTER 35

FOR THE LAST WEEK AND HALF THE COMMUNITY EXISTED IN
something akin to a fog. People wandered about, going about their
chores and pretending that life was going on. But Barbara had no
interest in washing dishes or sweeping floors, so she stayed outside.
She preferred it out there, away from the others and their awkward
attempts at solace.

I know how you feel.

He's in a better place now.

Everything happens for a reason.

Fuck them and their hackneyed comfort.

She's rather be alone than subject herself to that nonsense. At
least outside she could cry when she wanted. Yell when she wanted.
Drink when she wanted.

It seemed Myrtle, with her bottomless supply of booze, was the
only person who knew how to numb the pain.

That was something to be grateful for at least.

She strolled toward the graves, toward Richard's plot. It had been
a little more than a week and the ground had settled, leaving a slight
hollow in front of the wooden cross that marked his final resting

place. She told herself she ought to get the wheelbarrow and a few shovelfuls of dirt so she could level it out, but she didn't have the gumption.

Instead she flopped onto the earth beside him and pulled the silver flask from her pocket. It was almost empty. Just a few swallows left. Soon she'd have to go inside and raid Myrtle's stash, but for now she would nurse it.

After years of mourning her husband she'd allowed herself to picture a new future. A life where she was more than a nagging mother. A world where someone who didn't share her blood could love her. What a joke that had been.

Nothing was going to bring him back but being outside she could at least hold on to a part of him, of something, that reminded her that she was still a person.

The sound of hurried footsteps on the pavement woke her from her melancholy daydream. A group of men, the new guards, ran toward the gate.

"Open it up!" One of the men screamed. And just like that, the others were pulling the doors open to the wall.

Curiosity got the best of her and Barbara stood, stepping away from the grave. She wondered if the protectors were back. It surprised her to realize she was excited at the thought of seeing Wyatt again. Not because she didn't care, but because nothing these days could lift the cloud of despair that clung to her like heavy fabric.

As Barbara neared the gate, she realized this was no celebratory event.

A lone man staggered toward the community. He looked like walking death.

"Shit, it's Clark," Barbara heard one of the guards say.

"Jesus Christ get him some water!" another yelled.

And then she recognized him. Clark was one of the soldiers. His camo fatigues were saturated with blood. His face was sunken. His lips blistered. A filthy sock was tied around his throat like a scarf.

"What happened, man?" A guard asked, his voice panicked.

"Ambush... Total clusterfuck." The words sounded like meat pushed through crushed glass.

"Get him too med bay, now!" One of the guards shouted.

The men grabbed Clark under the arms and by the legs, carrying like a soldier being hurried off a battlefield and, Barb thought, that was about right.

If he was in such awful shape, what did that mean for Wyatt. And the others. Why was this man, who looked moments away from death, alone?

Barb felt her stomach tighten. She knew why. A woman who'd dealt with as much grief in her life as she had could see death coming like an air traffic controller bringing in a 737.

But it couldn't be true. Not Wyatt.

The guard rushed Clark toward the casino and their path went straight past Barbara. As they moved by the man's head lolled to the side and he saw her. His eyes widened. She thought he looked like he might cry if he had any moisture in his body, but he looked as dried out as a scarecrow that had spent decades in the field.

"Sorry," he said. "Tried to save him." He coughed or choked; it was hard to tell the difference. "Your boy died a hero."

With that they were gone.

Barbara felt her knees go weak and her head swim and she passed out.

CHAPTER 36

Seth wheeled himself down the halls as fast as he could push. He couldn't believe what the men had said.

Was his brother really dead? It had to be bad info. Some stupid fucker misheard and spread gossip that wasn't true. Because Wyatt wasn't supposed to die.

If Papa was right about everything, God and all, then how could God let this happen?

Then he remembered what Papa had said at the mass funeral.

Nothing was guaranteed in this life.

Was he right about that?

He could hear commotion as he neared the medical bay. A flurry of raised voices frantic and panicked.

When he got to the room, he saw Franklin and an older, balding man whose remaining hair was snow white. Seth remembered his name was Jose and that he'd been put in charge of medical after Ramona's death in the attack.

Franklin sorted through a cabinet, checking labels on bottles while Jose used scissors to cut the sock off Clark's neck. The soldier was sprawled awkwardly on a cart, one of his legs hanging off the side. Seth thought he looked more dead than alive.

"I don't even know what I'm looking for," Franklin said.

"Anything ending in 'cillin. This bastard's burning up. Must be full of infection."

Franklin glanced back at them. "What about that fucking hole in his neck? Should we even waste the antibiotics?"

They weren't equipped for any of this, Seth thought.

"We aren't equipped for this," Jose said, and despite the chaos Seth was pleased to be a step ahead, as usual. "I can try to stitch it up but I'm not promising anything. Shit, I can't even sew on a button."

"Mom," Seth muttered to himself. She'd be able to help with the stitching part if nothing else.

He wheeled back down the hallway, arms burning, but he didn't need to go far. Barbara was already there. Her clothes were covered in a thin layer of dust, but she looked calm. No, not calm, Seth realized. His mother looked blank. Empty. Like the lights were on but no one was home.

"Mom, you have to take a look at Clark. He was shot in the neck or something and needs stitches," Seth said. "We need to fix him up so he can tell us where to find Wyatt."

At the sound of Wyatt's name, she looked down to Seth. "Wyatt?" She said. "He's dead."

Seth couldn't hear that. Not now. He grabbed her hand, pulling her down the hall. "Just come on."

Barbara followed him, trance-like, until they returned to the medical bay.

Franklin and Jose had been joined by a few guards, but everyone looked clueless. Seth wondered why Papa wasn't here, if for nothing else than to tell them all to get their heads out of their asses.

"Move over, my mom can help him," Seth commanded.

All the men looked relieved. Now someone else could take the blame when things inevitably went wrong.

"Get her a needle and some thread," Seth said.

Jose did as told. He handed the items to Barbara who accepted them but didn't react otherwise. The men all stared at her, at the frozen shell of a woman.

"Stitch him up, mom." Seth gave her a gentle push in the hip.

"I used to do alterations in Portland," Barbara said, her words dreamy and light. "Wedding dresses mostly."

"I remember," Seth said. "Now you need to close the wound on Clarks neck."

Barbara finally looked down at Clark and seemed to regain a small part of herself. "Okay," she said. A little more came back. "Get some iodine first. We need to clean it up before I can stitch it."

Franklin passed Jose a bottle of orange liquid. Jose sprayed it into Clark's neck wound and roughly swabbed it with a fistful of cotton. Clark gave a low moan. "Cocksucker."

Barbara closed the wound in short order. Neat, precise stitches. Seth was proud of her for coming through when needed but noticed. She was more alert now and her gaze had shifted to Clark's torso where a hole and a large, maroon stain were all too evident.

She took the scissors she'd use to cut the suture thread to slice off Clark's shirt, then pulled it open.

Everyone in the room gasped.

Seth's medical experience was limited to TV dramas and the occasional horror movie, but he knew what he was looking at.

Clark was going to die.

A fist-sized hole marred his stomach and from it stretched red streaks. It seeped puke green pus and, through the hole Seth, could see coils of intestines which were black and swollen.

There was another hole at his side. This one was smaller, but an inch of wood protruded from it. After a moment, Seth realizes it was the shaft of an arrow. Which meant that more of the arrow was still inside the man.

"Do something," Franklin said, his voice too hard for Seth's taste.

Barbara turned her attention from Clark's destroyed body to

Franklin's bossy face. "There's nothing to do but make him comfortable. Do you have any pain killers?"

Jose shook his head. "I don't know." He began the hunt.

Seth wheeled up to Clark, as close as he could. The smell of rot coming off the man almost made him sick. "Clark, this is Seth. Wyatt's brother. You have to tell me what happened."

Clark opened his eyes a little wider and met Seth's. "The cripple?" He asked.

Seth nodded. "Yeah. I'm the cripple. Now what about Wyatt?"

Clark rocked his head side to side. "Got him with spears. Arrows. I lost count."

"Where is he?" Seth demanded.

"Dead." Clark said. "They're all dead."

Jose returned to the table with a syringe and a small bottle. He held it up like it was a Cracker Jack prize. "I found this. Oxymorphone. How much should I give him?" He asked Barbara.

Barbara turned away from all of them and walked toward the exit. "All of it," she said, and Seth watched her leave.

CHAPTER 37

Papa stood at the head of the dwindling group of men and women who called the casino home and recited his rote homily. Allie thought he sounded like the teacher in the old Charlie Brown cartoons. *Wah wah wah wah wah.*

He meant well, but she didn't want to hear it. She didn't want promises of better days ahead or how this was all part of God's plan.

Wyatt was dead.

There was nothing that could be said that would make her feel better. Nothing that could calm her down. Nothing that could make anything different.

The last time they were together they fought. She was so demeaning. And now he was never coming back.

Spread out before the remaining residents were three rows of crosses, all lined up beside the graves still fresh from the attack on the casino. Only there was no disturbed dirt in front of these new crosses. Except for one. Because the only body to bury was Clark's.

There was chatter about building a monument to the fallen protectors, but first they wanted to gather mementos and trinkets from the fallen. Wyatt, Alexander, and the others. Allie supposed she should bother to find out their names since they died horribly, just like the man she thought she might love. But she couldn't care less about any of them. That was rude. She knew that. But it was the truth and she wouldn't apologize for her feelings.

The crowd began to disperse, and Allie realized the funeral was over. Time to move on and pretend like it never happened.

She caught Franklin staring her way and acknowledged him with a nod. He offered a pitying, half smile. The kind that people used in times like these when they wanted to be reassuring but knew the situation was fucked.

"How are you holding up?" He asked.

Allie shrugged. "About as well as can be expected, I suppose."

"It still doesn't seem real. Like they aren't really gone," he said.

"It's real enough" Allie felt like her skin was going to crawl off her arms and squeezed her hands together to hold it in place.

"They're having a meal on the veranda. It's not for everyone, just friends of the de-- Fallen. Will you come?" Franklin shifted on his feet and, for the first time, Allie thought he looked nervous.

"I'm sorry, but I'm really not up for it."

"It would be cathartic. Shared pain and all that. I think it would be good for you too."

The last thing she wanted was to be around people right now, but Franklin was being so kind it felt rude to decline. "Okay. But I'm only staying for a little while."

"You can stay as long or as little as you want, Allie."

She followed him, but her mind was still consumed with everything she'd lost.

CHAPTER 38

It had been over a month since Wyatt's death and, as Seth looked at his mother, he realized she was getting worse instead of better. The initial shock seemed to have worn off and that void had been replaced with a sadness unlike anything Seth had seen before.

She was even more despondent than when his father never came home from Boston. That was bad, but she had two young sons to care for and to distract her. Plus, the world was crashing down around them which probably kept her grief at bay. Now, in the relative calm of life at the casino, she had nothing to occupy her mind but thinking about everything she'd lost.

That, and alcohol.

As he looked at her across the table, Seth thought she might fall off her chair. Her spaghetti remained uneaten on her plate and she swayed side to side, eyes half-closed. Like a woman in a lounge chair aboard a luxury yacht.

"I can get you something different if you aren't up for Italian night," he said

Barbara blinked in slow motion. "Not hungry, hon. You want it?"

Seth shook his head. "I'm fine. But you need to eat."

He wondered how he'd become the parent in this situation. And he resented this new role. Because as much as he pitied her for her losses, she still had him. She still had a living son.

That didn't seem to matter these days. He couldn't recall one hundred words she'd spoken to him since they learned Wyatt had died and that only reinforced something he'd believed all his life.

Wyatt was the favorite son.

Growing up he'd felt loved, but not special. Cared for, but not appreciated. And after he ended up in the chair, he became a worry and a burden while Wyatt emerged as the hero for being so willing to care for him.

Now, he wondered if she even loved Richard, a man she'd known for just a few weeks, more than him. Than her own child. He'd watched as she spent days crying by his grave, meanwhile she never once bothered to ask Seth how he was doing, how he was holding up.

He felt like his entire life prior to coming to the casino had been a waste. And it made him realize how much he needed Papa and his love.

"I'm going back to my room," Seth said to his mother.

Barbara gave a weak nod.

"You're sure there's nothing I can get you to eat?"

She didn't respond at all to that, so he turned his chair away from the table and left her alone with her sadness.

As he wheeled himself along, he thought about the last few weeks and how he handled everything. Overall, he was impressed with how he'd done.

It wasn't that he didn't miss Wyatt. If anything, it was the opposite. He missed him like he missed being able to walk. He didn't simply love his brother, he depended on him.

Wyatt was his strength when he was weak. His heart when he was despondent. Wyatt was the one who got him through all of life's hardships and now he was gone, and Seth had to find a way to get by.

And he made it.

On his own Seth had his chance to emerge from his brother's

shadow. And he had. People here came to him for advice and guidance. They prayed with him as they coped with their anxiety and fear. They trusted him. Loved him. Respected him.

It wasn't just Papa that believed in him anymore. *He* believed in himself. He saw himself maturing, getting stronger. He was leading the community, just as Papa was training him to do.

With his brother dying Seth felt like he could be himself for the first time. But thinking that made him feel lower than dogshit.

He hoped that guilt would go away soon, because he didn't deserve it. It was only the truth.

CHAPTER 39

These days Allie's mind wavered between anger over having lost Wyatt so soon and gratitude that they hadn't had more time together. Because more time meant more love, more memories, and a bigger hole.

She longed for him, but life could always be worse, and she tried to remind herself of that each and every day.

Franklin had been so good to her, helping her through the pain, listening when she wanted to talk, and just being there when she didn't.

He made her get out of bed when all she wanted to do was sleep, made her connect with others in the community, made her go on living.

It was because of Franklin that she didn't end up like Barbara - a broken, miserable mess.

"I know I'll never replace him. I'm not trying to. And I'm not trying to force you into anything. I'm just asking you to give me a chance," Franklin said.

She inspected him as they sat in the courtyard. His handsome, earnest face reminded her of a dog in a shelter, desperate for a new home. *Pick me, pick me.* Allie knew she owed him, so why was it so hard to just do what Franklin was asking?

He deserved a chance after everything he'd done for her. And she was attracted to him. Who wouldn't be? It should be easy. But it wasn't.

The memory of Wyatt always lingered in her thoughts. He'd been the one to save her. He'd been the one to give her a real chance at life. Then he got himself killed.

Part of her was still angry that he went into the desert when she begged him not too. That he'd thrown away his life when she pleaded with him to stay. Was she supposed to sacrifice the rest of her life when he was the one who left her?

"I know I need to let him go. But I just need more time."

Franklin nodded. He really was so patient with her, so understanding. "I get it, Allie. And I'm not telling you to forget about Wyatt, please believe me when I say that."

"I do."

He reached out, his fingers brushing her forearm. "I just can't stand seeing you hurting."

She felt her heartbeat quicken. What had she done to deserve such kind, compassionate men in her life?

Allie chewed on her lip; not sure she could get the words out but gave it her best shot. "I tell you what, let's have dinner together tonight. Not in the cafeteria with everyone else. On one of the balconies. Just the two of us."

Franklin's eyes gleamed. "Only if you're sure."

As if she could possibly change her mind after seeing the excitement on his face. "I am."

She knew she was blessed that someone so genuine, so accepting, and she wouldn't deny it - so handsome - wanted to be with her. But she fought back tears as she remembered Wyatt's face.

It had been more than a month now, but she could remember every centimeter of him. The chicken pox scar on his jaw. The patchy bit of stubble that sprouted from his chin. The way the left side of his mouth twitched when he tried to hide a grin.

Their time together had been short, but it was so crammed full of memories. And now those memories were all she had.

But there came a time to move on and make new memories.

CHAPTER 40

PAPA LAID SPRAWLED ON THE BED, LOOKING HEAVIER THAN ever. Since the protectors had been wiped out, the big man sometimes spent days in his bedroom, only leaving to use the toilet. Seth worried about his health, both physically and mentally.

Belle, one of Papa's wives, laid at his side and fed him canned fruit one spoonful at a time.

"Jorge Bolivar has volunteered to recruit a new group of protectors," Seth said, glancing at his notes.

Every day he made it his mission to speak with each member of the community to check on them and ensure they knew they were being cared for and listened to. Recently, he noticed many had begun to worry for their safety, feeling that they were sitting ducks should the cannibals decide to renew their attacks. It didn't help matters that Papa hadn't spoken in public in weeks.

Papa craned his head to the side to look at Seth. His lips were parted, and partially masticated fruit dribbled from the gap. "I don't see that's necessary. Long as we keep the gates manned. We're safe inside."

Belle wiped Papa's mouth with the bedsheet. "Thank you, my love," he said.

She nodded silent.

"I trust your judgment, Papa," Seth said. Although, as much as he tried to convince himself otherwise, there were times that he had reservations.

"Anything else of which I should be aware?"

Seth looked back at his notes. "Not really. I do think the people who like to hear from you. Maybe tomorrow--"

Papa waved his hand, dismissive. "Remind them that patience sews a bountiful harvest. Yahweh bestows peace upon those who comprehend."

Seth didn't think that even made sense. "They miss you, Papa."

"And I them. And I them."

Belle fed Papa another mouthful of fruit. He chewed, breathing heavy. Seth thought it might be time to leave, to let his mentor rest, but then Papa erupted into a gagging fit. He rolled onto his side and regurgitated the food onto the white duvet. Seth saw putrid phlegm and dark blood intermixed with the vomit and his worries multiplied by a factor of ten.

"Oh dear. I've gone and soiled the bed like a toddler," Papa said. "Belle would you please get a wet cloth?"

She was up and gone without a word, but Seth struggled to keep his eyes off the mess.

"Look at me, my son," Papa said.

Seth did and when his gaze shifted to Papa, he was relieved to see the man looked a bit more alert than he had in some time.

"I understand your concerns. I have been lax in my responsibilities of late. To everyone, but especially to you."

Seth shook his head. "You don't feel well. I understand. You need to rest and heal."

"My body betrays me," Papa said. "But my mind and my spirit are tack sharp. And I accept the concerns of our brothers and sisters.

You must tell them I appreciate their patience and that their reward is coming."

Seth waited, sensing there was more. He was right.

"Tell them it is time for the tombola."

Seth furrowed his brow. Was this more nonsense? "I don't know what that is."

Papa laughed. "Of course you don't. It's been years since our last. Far too long." He pushed himself up in bed, resting his back against the headboard. "The tombola is a celebration unlike any other. It is our way of proving our love and devotion to Yahweh. Of showing Him that we are His obedient servants. Of proving and renewing our faith."

All of that sounded perfect to Seth. The community needed something, and this sounded like the answer to their prayers.

"How do we go about it?" Seth asked.

"Fetch Franklin for me. He knows the ceremony well. And inform the community that we shall be hosting the tombola this weekend. And to prepare."

"And you'll be there?" Seth asked.

Papa smiled, looking more like himself than he had in weeks. "Of course, of course, my child. I would not dare miss it."

CHAPTER 41

THE HUMMING WAS JOYLESS AND OUT OF TUNE. THE NOISE A man makes out of habit rather than purpose.

He tried to place it, to decide whether it was a song, a hymn, or only a made-up tune. But soon he lost interest.

All he could remember was pain. In his chest, his stomach, his head. It had consumed the entirety of him and made anything else, even the act of thinking, impossible.

Now, to his surprise and relief, he could think again. And rather than waste time trying to decipher the mystery music, he had a more important question to answer.

Where the hell was, he?

He sat up. Or tried. His body was tied down. He strained his arms, kicked his legs, with no results.

He turned his head from side to side but saw nothing but darkness. Only, that wasn't quite true. There were random blobs and shapes hidden in a dense fog that made them impossible to decipher.

When he opened his mouth to call out, he felt like his jaw had been glued shut for years. It gave with an audible pop, admitting a gasp of dry air that sent him into an immediate coughing fit.

Through his own racket he heard movement. Someone walking, approaching.

The darkness gave way to murky illumination, but he still couldn't see anything other than shapes.

But he could sense he was no longer alone. And that realization brought with it no relief because he didn't know who was holding him captive.

The musky, masculine smell of body odor invaded his nose. And then he felt a touch against his face. He flinched, but his retreat was limited to a few inches.

"Hold still now. I covered your eyes because you kept 'em open too often. Made me afraid they might dry out and shrivel up in this torrefied hellscape."

A pair of hands fumbled, fingers fidgeting, and then he felt a cloth that had been tied around his head come loose.

And he could see. Almost. The rapid shift from dark to bright blinded him and he squeezed his eyelids closed. That didn't help much as light stabbed its way through and he instinctively tried to cover them with his hand, forgetting about his tethers.

"Those were for your own well-being. Don't you be getting the wrong idea about me now." More fumbling fingers. "A restless one you were. Made me afeared you'd dislodge your IV."

His hands came free. Then his legs.

His first instinct was to sit up, but that brought with it a thunder-clap of pain.

"You might ought to take it easy for a spell. Let yourself accli-mate. You've been insentient for a long while."

His eyes began to adjust, the blinding brightness became tolera-ble, normal. And he saw the man who hunkered beside him.

The hermit.

He shared a rueful smile, then spat a mouthful of chewing tobacco onto the floor. "I'm Gerald. And I never did catch your name, newcomer."

"Wyatt," he said, although his mouth was still as dry as sand.

Gerald patted him on the thigh. "Nice to meet you. Sit there for a few minutes while I put on some coffee. Then we'll talk."

He stood and left the room and left Wyatt to wonder what the hell had happened to him.

"I never saw a man as close to dead as you were who found a way to fight back. Not sure if that makes you resilient or obstinate," Gerald sipped his coffee.

Wyatt did the same, trying not to let on how terrible it tasted. He could discern no coffee flavor, instead finding only dirt and possibly shit. But he didn't want to be rude and even this foul-tasting concoction was welcome against his parched throat. "Maybe some of both?"

Gerald nodded. "That sounds accurate."

He'd already told Wyatt about finding him washed ashore beside the creek. Told him how he thought he was dead, until he kept bleeding. Told him how he'd brought him back to his settlement in a wheelbarrow (the same one on which Wyatt had cut his hand). And told him how he cleaned out his wounds and sewed them closed.

They were still at the beginning though, and Wyatt had the feeling there was much more to share.

"After 48 hours I had the feeling you might stick around, but you were comatose, so my concern shifted to keeping you hydrated. I concocted some saline solution by boiling water and salt and hooked you up to a drip. Not all that different from my irrigation emitters when you think about it."

The thought of being kept alive in this shack by a man who thought of him as akin to a tomato made goosebumps flare on Wyatt's flesh and he folded his arms to conceal them.

"Your pyrexia was uncontrollable for the first week. Must have been full of infection from whatever the cannibals shot into you. I truly believed I'd find you expired every time I checked in, but you muddled through." Gerald tilted his cup toward him in a toasting gesture.

Wyatt mimicked him and both drank. But there was one question Wyatt needed answered before he could embrace the celebration. "That was a week ago, you said?"

Gerald's proud smile faltered. He covered well, but Wyatt knew something was up. "No, Wyatt. It was considerably longer than that."

"How much longer?" He'd felt the facial hair that had sprouted across his chin and jaw. There was even something resembling a mustache on his upper lip. He rarely went more than three days without shaving, even when they were on the road, so it was difficult to estimate how long it would take to get this furry.

"Let's see..." Gerald set his coffee cup aside and stood, turning his back as he shuffled through some journals. He found the one he wanted and opened it. He turned page after page before stopping.

"Well?" Wyatt asked.

"It appears you've been cohabitating with me the better part of 51 days."

Wyatt felt his stomach drop. Almost two months? How was that possible? He jumped to his feet. That was a mistake as pain raged. He stumbled, putting a hand on the nearest wall to steady himself.

"Settle, please. You're still recovering. It's impossible to know the amount of internal damage you sustained."

"I have to get home," Wyatt said.

"No," Gerald said. "What you have to do is rest and eat and get your strength back. You've been living on saltwater and pureed vegetable smoothies for nearly two months. If you leave here now, you'll expire from exhaustion before you go a mile."

That wasn't what Wyatt wanted to hear, but his body told him it was the reality of his situation. And what good would it have done to survive the attack only to die alone in the desert?

"Alright. Then can I please have something to eat?"

"Of course." Gerald nodded.

CHAPTER 42

OVER THE FOLLOWING TWO WEEKS, WYATT GORGED HIMSELF ON the riches of Gerald's garden. He's never been big on veggies as a kid, but now he couldn't get enough of the stuff. It was as if his body was screaming for nutrients and minerals and, given the choice, he'd have turned down a truckload of Cheetos for a few ripe tomatoes.

He felt bad for eating so much of Gerald's food, but the man was willing, even eager, to share. He seemed to enjoy the company and Wyatt shared that opinion. Although the man was eccentric, maybe even a little squirrely, he seemed more relatable than most of the folks at the casino. There were no airs, no pretenses. Life with Gerald seemed almost normal.

Wyatt guessed he'd put on twenty pounds since emerging from the coma. The ribcage which had poked so notoriously against his skin was now hidden. And the six pack he'd developed during his slumber was gone. He didn't miss it.

He'd been helping Gerald around the property. Fixing his fence, harvesting crops. It was the least he could do, after all. As each day passed, he felt stronger and more energetic. And, more eager to get back to his family.

Because, as much as he enjoyed the quiet life at Gerald's shack, he missed his mother and brother. Allie and Supper. And he wondered if they were safe. Two months was a long time in this wretched excuse for a world and he worried some other terrible thing might have happened.

He needed to move on, and Gerald must have known it was coming because, the next day, Wyatt awoke to a hiker's backpack filled with food. The man himself was nowhere to be seen, so Wyatt slung the pack over his shoulder and left the shack in search of the man to whom he owed his life.

He found Gerald digging a hole for a fence post at the edge of the property. Sweat slicked his body, but dust had mixed in with the moisture to form a paste. Wyatt thought he looked a little like a suburban housewife getting a mud mask beauty treatment, but Gerald was far from beautiful.

"Suppose you're heading out." Gerald plunged his shovel into the ground and let it stand upright.

Wyatt nodded. "Yeah. It's time."

The man sat down in the dirt. "I could see it in your eyes. You can only keep a horse in a stable so long. And you're ready now. Physically, anyway."

The last comment made Wyatt curious. "You don't think I've got my head on straight?"

Gerald patted the earth beside him. Wyatt wanted to get on, but he also couldn't be rude, so he took a seat. "You're bereft of vital information. And if you'll humor an old man, I'd like to educate you before you go on your merry way."

Gerald passed Wyatt a dented canteen. Wyatt took a drink, gasping when he realized it was whisky and not water. The old man gave a low chuckle. "My own recipe," he said.

"So, what do you need to tell me, Gerald? I'm all ears." Wyatt's hand drifted to the ear which had been shot way back in Big Josh's town, tracing his fingers over the ragged bits. He wondered how many more times he'd be able to dodge death.

"That casino you call home. It's not the mecca you think it is. More of a mirage if you ask me."

"Did Alexander tell you about it?"

"No," Gerald said. "I know because I was the founder of that place."

That didn't sound possible at all. To the people at the casino, Gerald was a nut living in the wild. "Papa said he--"

"Pfft. Papa." Gerald spat into the dirt. "Who calls themselves that anyway? No sane person, let me tell you."

That part Wyatt could agree with.

"I saved that fat charlatan's life. And back then his name was Bernie. And he was a glorified maid. Or, I'm sorry *entrepreneur*." He made air quotes with his fingers. "Bernie didn't know God from a gopher back then."

Wyatt decided to take another drink of the whisky. He had a feeling he'd need it by the time this story was done.

"When the bombs hit, I was a pastor and some of my congregation and I started going door to door looking for survivors. I found Bernie, half-buried under the fallen roof of his house. His family was there. All dead. But he survived. I thought it was a miracle then. Time has changed my opinion on that, however.

"The suburbs were gone, everything either destroyed or burning. So, we sought out somewhere people could be safe. Where they could be loved and heal. Where we could all work together and become stronger.

"Bernie seemed to be the same as all the others, at first. He listened to my sermons. Took part in our prayers and worship sessions. I was proud of him, Wyatt. And, though I'm loath to admit it, I was proud of myself because I'd saved not only his life but his soul. I led him to God, you see, and for a pastor that's one of the greatest gifts. But I was punished for my pride."

Wyatt shifted, uncomfortable with where this was going as he knew it was nowhere good. He wondered if he could believe everything this man was telling him, but he couldn't see a reason why Gerald would lie.

"Bernie studied the good book and learned the Word of God better than me. He started his own worship groups in the community - Papa's Prayer Warriors, he called them. I was pleased at first. Until I sat in on one of his services." He reached for the canteen. "Give me that."

Wyatt did and Gerald took a long swallow.

"You see, Bernie perverted God's word. He pulled things from the bible, especially the old testament, and twisted it all. I don't know if it was watching his family die in front of him, or maybe the fallout was rotting his brain or maybe he was just plain wicked, but it was horrifying to listen to the way he spouted fire and brimstone and sacrifices and offerings. There was nothing about Christ in his sermons. It was all about fear and revenge. Fucker."

Wyatt raised a questioning eyebrow. Gerald saw it and smiled.

"I used to be a pastor. Doesn't mean I'm not still human." His smile quickly left his face. "While I preached love, Bernie promised retribution. And, I'm sad to say, his voice was stronger. The community gravitated toward him and embraced his message."

"You couldn't stop him?" Wyatt asked.

"Fighting is not my way. God gave us all free will. The choice was theirs to make and they made it."

"Did they throw you out?"

"Nothing that dramatic. One morning I packed my suitcase and left. I wanted no part of what that place had become."

Wyatt remained silent for a long minute.

"You're disappointed in me," Gerald said.

"No. I..." Wyatt struggled to find the right response.

"It's fine. I'm disappointed in myself." Gerald screwed the lid back onto the canteen. He set it aside and rose to his feet. He grabbed the shovel and resumed digging.

"Why'd you tell me all that?"

"Information is power, Wyatt. Now it's your turn to make a decision."

Wyatt stood. He shifted the pack into place. The pain in his body had alleviated to the greatest extent, but some lingered. He had a feeling that would last a long while. "I have family. I can't just leave them."

"Then God help you," Gerald said. "Because I won't."

Wyatt understood his man's position, but he wasn't going to run like Gerald did.

CHAPTER 43

Allie felt Franklin's hardness as he pressed against her. His hands were all over her in a way that felt more like an excavation than a romantic interlude. His mouth sucked at her neck; his lips dragged across her cheeks. Only well-timed dodges kept his tongue from ending up in her mouth.

But that was coming soon enough. Because Franklin was wound up and raring to go and blind to her body language. And she didn't have the heart to tell him out loud to stop. To keep his desperate paws to himself. To tell him to fuck off.

Had she led him on, she wondered. Sent messages that he misinterpreted? She was sure she hadn't but that desperate need to be nice, to avoid confrontation with the man who'd shown her nothing but kindness since she came to the casino, kept her from speaking up.

Just put up with it, she told herself.

Her eyes drifted across the desert, desperate to send her mind somewhere else while Franklin did whatever he was going to do to her. Why aren't there stars, she wondered. If there were stars, I could make a wish.

But what would she wish for? For Franklin to come to his senses?

For the world to be normal again? For Wyatt to come back and save her yet again.

The last one, she thought. Definitely the last one.

No matter how much she told her she was over his death, that she was ready to move on, her heart refused to let go.

Why'd you leave me, Wyatt? Why didn't you come back?

A few floors below the balcony where she was trapped with Franklin, Allie heard the guards shouting to each other, but she couldn't make out their words. Just random mumbles against the silence of the dead world.

At least their noises gave her a distraction as Franklin's hands found their way under her shirt.

It'll be over soon enough, she told herself.

Franklin spoke too. Passionate ramblings that he probably thought were romantic or seductive, but she found cloying.

"You're so damn sexy, Allie. I never met anyone as hot as you. I want you so bad I feel like I'm going to explode."

Wyatt never felt the need for such hollow utterances. His words had always been genuine. Tender.

At the fence below, the guards were now down from their perches. The four of them had gathered at the gate. Their voices were louder, their tones more anxious, but their words still indecipherable.

Franklin's walkie-talkie, which lied on the table beside their leftovers, crackled.

"Franklin, this is Jorge. Come in."

Thank God, Allie thought. This is my out. He'll have to attend to some issue, and I can run back to my room, lock the door, and hide the rest of the night.

But Franklin didn't let up. His hands squeezed her breasts. Fingers spun her nipples like they were dials on a radio.

Maybe he thinks that's the way to turn me on, she thought, and almost laughed out loud.

"Franklin. Come in. Someone's approaching the gate," the voice on the walkie said.

"Fuck!" Franklin withdrew his hands from under her clothes. He moved to the table and grabbed the radio. "What?"

"There's a man about forty yards out."

Franklin looked to her. "Wait here, okay? This won't take long."

Allie wasn't about to obey. "Alright," she lied. She'd deal with the consequences in the morning.

Franklin brought the walkie to his lips. "I'll be down in two minutes."

He clipped the radio to his belt and as he turned away from her, Allie heard words that couldn't be true. Words she must have imagined.

"Holy shit! It looks like Wyatt!"

She saw Franklin's body tense. He didn't acknowledge the transmission, instead doubling his pace and leaving her.

Allie spun toward the balcony, staring at the open land. She squinted, trying to focus, but couldn't see anyone outside the fence.

Don't get your hopes up, she told herself. If you don't expect anything you can't get hurt. Because what she thought she heard couldn't be true. If Jorge had said Wyatt's name, he was wrong. It had been two months. Too long. Wyatt was dead.

But what if he wasn't? What if Wyatt really had returned to save her one more time?

CHAPTER 44

"Who goes there?" The voice asked.

Wyatt didn't recognize it and was almost scared to answer. For all he knew cannibals had taken over the casino and wiped out everyone else. Of course, if that was the case, he'd just as soon be dead anyway.

"Wyatt Morrill." He continued walking, closing in on the gate hoping there'd be someone who'd recognize him.

"Bullshit," the same voice said. "He's dead."

"Not quite. Not yet anyway." He'd been walking almost nonstop since leaving Gerald's and his still recovering body was exhausted.

Soon, the guards were visible. Their faces were of the ring a bell variety, but he knew none of their names. He realized there must have been quite an adjustment at the casino, and he wondered if any of the other protectors made it back.

Wyatt saw Franklin rush from the casino, beelining it toward the guards. He grabbed a pair of binoculars and stared. Even without visual aids, Wyatt saw Franklin's expression change. It wasn't shock or relief. It was anger.

After seeing the look on Franklin's face, Wyatt half expected the man to give orders to shoot. He slowed from a jog to a slow trot, not eager to run toward a bullet.

As Franklin leaned into one of the guards Wyatt held his breath. Then, the gate opened.

Wyatt hadn't made it three steps past the fence when Allie collided with him, knocking out his breath and robbing him of any chance to say the words he'd planned all through the return hike. The floral aroma of her body wash made him realize how bad he must stink but she didn't seem to mind. Her arms were around him, her lips against his.

"Wyatt, I love you," she said in between kissing his scruffy face.

It was one hell of a homecoming.

AFTER HIS RETURN WYATT WAS SHUTTLED TO THE MEDICAL BAY where Jose, the new doctor, made a show of examining his myriad of injuries. Even though all of them were healing well, the man muttered about the poor quality of the stitchwork and said, at least a dozen times, "I don't know how you're still alive."

Wyatt had little patience for being put on display for this man who, before Ramona's death, had been one of the cooks and whose medical experience amounted to working as an orderly at a personal care home.

He reached for his shirt, ready to redress and move on, when one of the doors opened.

His mother stood on the doorway, frozen in place. Wyatt could see Seth behind her, and Allie behind him. It was about time.

"What are you waiting for," he asked them.

Barbara moved into the room, two shaky steps. She was a shadow of the woman he'd left and the smile that had come across his face when he saw her faded. How much more damage has this caused, he wondered. And he cursed himself for putting her through this mess.

Seth pushed his chair past her. Wyatt thought he seemed... disappointed? No, that wasn't right. He was just shocked, like everyone else.

What else changed over the last two months, Wyatt wondered. At least Allie was the same. But even that wasn't the whole truth. She was more beautiful than even when she came to him.

"Quit poking at him, Jose. He's fine." She helped Wyatt into his shirt. He didn't need assistance but didn't protest. The soft skin on his fingers brushed against his arms, causing them to break out in goosebumps.

He heard Franklin snort, or was it a cough? Then he saw Allie tuck her head. It seemed something was different there too, but he wasn't going to worry about that. She'd told him she loved him and that was all that mattered.

"You look good for a dead man, brother," Seth said as he rolled nearer.

"Is that a compliment?" Wyatt asked.

"I haven't decided."

Wyatt hopped off the gurney and went to tousle Seth's hair, but his little brother dodged out of the way, instead holding out his fist. Wyatt rapped their knuckles together, trying not to overthink the subdued greeting.

Barbara still clung to the edge of the room. She looked so unsteady on her feet that Wyatt thought she might be using the wall to remain upright. He decided that he was tired of waiting and went to her.

"I'm so sorry." He felt her hands trembling as he took them in his own.

"I'm afraid I'm going to wake up," Barbara said. "And find out this was an awful dream."

"What would be awful about me coming back?" He asked.

"The awful part would be realizing you're still gone." She squeezed his hands, perhaps to verify this was real.

"It's not a dream. I'm back. A little skinnier and with a few new scars. But I'm back."

She fell against him, sobbing silently. He put an arm around her shoulders, and he realized he wasn't the only one who'd lost weight. She was verging on skeletal and, from the smell of her breath, he suspected she'd been surviving on booze and cigarettes. He only hoped it wasn't too late for her to heal.

He wished he could tell them everything right now. That Papa wasn't who they thought he was. The real story of the beginning of the casino. But Wyatt couldn't tell anyone that here, with prying eyes and eavesdropping ears. He'd have to wait until the time was right and only hoped that wasn't too far off.

CHAPTER 45

Two new bodyguards flanked Papa. They looked every bit as wide and dense as the original braindead bruiser twins and Wyatt wondered if there was some sort of meathead cloning operation going on in the basement.

He made a mental note to check once things settled down.

"Tell me now, Wyatt. What happened to everyone? What happened to Alexander?" Papa asked.

Wyatt cleared his throat. He knew these questions were inevitable, but he didn't want to relive that day.

"We marched straight into an ambush. Never had a chance." Wyatt drifted into his memories, remembering the screams, the sight of his friend's slow, brutal demise. The gurgling cries as they cut his head off. Wyatt felt his eyes burn. "They got Alexander first. After that it was chaos."

"It's alright. You're safe now," Papa said, placing his hand atop Wyatt's.

"I know. I just... It was a massacre. They didn't deserve that."

"No, they didn't. They were good people, each and every one of them. And they died heroes."

Wyatt thought that trite. They hadn't died like heroes. They died panicked and afraid. They died badly. If there was such a thing as a hero's death, it wasn't that.

"Clark got me to the river. They were chasing us. Shooting us. I went into the water and don't remember anything between that and a few days ago."

Wyatt swallowed hard. "Did he..." He knew the odds were slim but had to ask.

"He lived long enough to get back here to tell everyone that you were dead. That everyone was dead," Seth said. "That's why we didn't bother with a rescue party."

"I'm glad you didn't. Sending anyone into cannibal country is a death sentence." Wyatt swallowed hard over what he needed to say next. "Going out there was a mistake, Papa. And this eye for an eye bullshit needs to end."

Wyatt looked at the other men in the room to judge their reaction. Seth looked disinterested. The guards, blank. Papa, benevolent as always. Franklin was the only one who showed any visible dismay about Wyatt volunteering his opinion. A sneer marred his face and he made no attempt to hide it.

"If you ask me, the mission wasn't the problem. The people were. Next time we won't send men who run," Franklin said.

Papa reached out with an unsteady hand and patted Franklin's waist in a calming gesture. "Easy, son. Of the four of us only one was there and witnessed the bloodshed firsthand."

"Funny how he was the only one to live," Franklin said. "Makes me wonder what really happened."

"Enough." Papa's voice was firm and left no room for further debate. Then he looked to Wyatt. "I can't imagine the trauma, son. How did you survive?" Papa asked.

"The hermit found me." He saw Papa's eyes narrow. Or maybe that was his imagination. Either way he made note to be careful with his words. "He pulled out the arrows and spears, cleaned my wounds, and stitched me up. Then I guess he waited for me to die, but I didn't."

"The guy we get our veggies from saved you?" Seth asked.

"Yeah. Crazy bastard, but he must be handy with a needle." He tapped his side where one of the largest wounds was still tender.

"Well I'll be, Papa said. "Yahweh certainly held you in his healing embrace."

Wyatt nodded. "Amen."

"Did the hermit ask for anything in return? He rarely gives without receiving," Papa said.

Wyatt knew it was a test, that Papa was trying to see what, if anything, Gerald had told him. "Not that he told me. But I don't think we shared more than ten words after I came around. The guy's..." He twirled his finger around his ear in the universal sign for *crazy*.

That made Papa laugh, as sick and unhealthy a sound as Wyatt ever heard. "Indeed! Indeed..." The big man motioned to a bottle of brandy. "Would you have a drink with me, Wyatt? To celebrate?"

He didn't wait for an answer and poured three shots. He passed one off to Seth then offered one to Wyatt.

Wyatt shook his head. "I better not. Still recovering."

Papa's glistened. "Very well. More for me." He drank down both shots back to back. "I'm not sure if you've heard the good word, but we're hosting a celebration which begins tomorrow and lasts through Sunday. Your return will make it even more meaningful."

"A celebration?" Wyatt repeated.

"Yes, it's time for the community to return to our roots. To show Yahweh that we are still on the path to righteousness and glory."

Wyatt looked from Papa to Seth, who twirled his empty glass between his fingers. Seth caught him staring and put on a smile. "Who doesn't love a party, right, brother?"

CHAPTER 46

As music blared and revelers surrounded him, Wyatt felt like every nerve in his body was a live wire. In his experience, ceremonies at the casino didn't end well but he prayed this would be different.

The whole community was gathered, although its numbers were smaller than ever. He never bothered to get a head count, but he believed they were down by half, if not more. Such a dramatic and disheartening change.

As in the demonstration which ended with Vern's agonizing death, the makeshift stage once again set in front of the hotel. Thankfully, there was no mysterious figure hidden underneath a tarp. Instead it was just Papa, Seth, Franklin, Wyatt and of course, two of Papa's guards.

Wyatt surveyed the crowd and settled his eyes upon Allie and Barbara. His mother looked marginally more alert, but her face was still a blank mask. He'd hoped her mood would improve once the reality that he was alive set in, but so far that wasn't the case. He was beginning to wonder if she'd ever be happy again.

Everyone else was near manic in their revelry. People danced and sang along with the music. They feasted on mediocre food. They laughed and cheered and celebrated.

The crowd hushed as Papa stood. He tapped the microphone, grinning as it gave a whine of feedback. "Guess it's on," he said.

All eyes were on the big man as he continued. "To kick off the tombola I have a very special announcement to make." His tone was jovial and excited. Carnival barker rather than serious preacher. "Last night Yahweh thought it proper to bring back to us one of our own!"

The crowd erupted.

"Now," Papa said, raising his arms to calm the masses. "You all know Wyatt was the one that saved my life back when we were attacked. And he risked his life to avenge our lost brethren.

"We believed all of our protectors were lost. That all of our heroes had fallen at the hands of the savages that have claimed the land outside our walls as their own. But we were wrong! And let me tell you, friends, I've never been so pleased to be wrong!"

Another round of cheers passed through the crowd.

Papa turned to Wyatt. "Wyatt Morrill has proven to be not only brave, but selfless, reliable, and pure of heart. He is a man we can all trust. And that is why, my children, I am now declaring Wyatt as the new Chief Protector of this community. Of *our* community!"

The crowd went wild, but Wyatt was completely blindsided. Papa had never asked, or even hinted, that he was to be named the head of security. And he wanted no part of it.

Now Papa had not only made the decision but made it in public, leaving him with no choice. The big man motioned for Wyatt to stand, to accept the adulation, so Wyatt did. He sidled up beside Papa, noticing that it felt like an inferno of heat radiated from his massive body.

"A little warning would have been nice," Wyatt whispered.

Papa laughed. "Yahweh's will is greater than that of man."

"Fucking bullshit," Franklin said. Wyatt swiveled his head and saw the man storming off the stage. And as much as he tried not to be petty, that gave him an obscene amount of glee. Maybe this gig wasn't so bad after all.

CHAPTER 47

AFTER WYATT HAD BEEN ANNOUNCED AS THE NEW PROTECTOR the party resumed, but all Allie could think about were the men in her life.

Fuck, what had she done?

Wyatt climbed down from the stage, looking out into the crowd. She knew that he was looking for her. But she didn't want to be found yet.

Franklin was pushing through the crowd, giving little concern to who he collided with and offering no apologies. She knew this was her fault. She'd promised him a chance, only to yank it away at the last moment.

And now Wyatt was getting all this attention. It was no wonder Franklin was upset.

This was her mess to clean up. But she didn't know where to start.

She chased after Franklin, stealing glanced back at Wyatt who pursued with a confused expression on his face. Allie was ecstatic he was back, but she felt so awful for what had happened while he was gone.

How was she supposed to know he was still alive after all that time?

She ducked deeper into the crowd. The last thing she wanted was to hurt anyone, but here she was, fucking it all up anyway. The celebration and music were all white noise to her. Just a baseline for her thoughts. She dodged partygoers, slipping through cracks in the crowd, moving as fast as possible when--

She collided with Wyatt. She looked up and found the face she'd dreamed about on so many nights since he'd disappeared. The face she loved.

"If I didn't know any better, I'd think you were trying to avoid me."

"I was." She let out a nervous laugh. "Wyatt, I need to tell you about some things that happened while you were gone. When I thought you were--"

He kissed her before she could finish. When he broke away, he was smiling.

"I don't care what happened. It doesn't matter because I love you, Allie."

All her worries drifted away. She squeezed him tight. "Don't go dying on me again, you hear me? I can't do this without you."

He embraced her, wrapping his arms around her back. This man that was nearly a decade younger than her but made her feel so safe. So loved.

"I don't plan on it."

"Good," she said and realized she was crying, her tears soaking into Wyatt's shirt.

When they separated, she looked past Wyatt and found Franklin watching them from the edge of the crowd. She knew this must be hard on him, but he had to see her side too, right? If he was half the man, she thought he was he'd realize that her love for Wyatt wasn't going to disappear in two months.

She was also aware how hard it was for men to separate their feelings and logic. And that scared her.

As she wondered how this was going to work out, Franklin did the most shocking thing she could have imagined.

He smiled. It was tinged with sadness, but she saw in his eyes that he understood.

Allie smiled back, then Franklin gave an approving, understanding nod. And she felt like she experienced her second miracle in less than 24 hours.

CHAPTER 48

After a full day of partying Seth was wasted and, for once, glad to be in the chair. As Rosario pushed him down the hall, his mind raced with possibilities as to what they could do in bed, to give this night a proper send off. However, the way his head was spinning meant he was as apt to pass out as soon as his body hit the mattress than perform any sexual acrobatics.

As they passed by Papa's room Seth heard voices. One in particular was loud and sounded drunk. Not that he was one to judge.

"How the fuck could you reward him?" The voice said. "He's not even one of us!"

"It'll be alright," Papa said. "You worry too much."

"He's playing you for a fool, old man. How can you not see that?"

"We should go," Rosario said over Seth's shoulder.

He'd almost forgotten she was there. "No, I want to hear this," Seth said.

"It's spying. If we get caught..."

Seth waved away her concerns and leaned in closer to the door.

"Franklin," Papa said. His voice was slow and steady. Serious. "You are walking a fine line right now. We've been together almost from the beginning. I consider you a very loyal ally and disciple. But I do not need to be told what I can and cannot allow. Do you understand me?"

Seth wasn't even in the room, but he could feel the tension.

When Franklin spoke again his tone had changed. Genial rather than accusatory. "I apologize Papa. You know that I would never tell you what to do," Franklin said.

Seth pictured him groveling on his knees, which caused him to let out a little laugh.

Papa continued. "I understand you're upset Franklin. You have every right to be. And I know your words were driven by anger toward him and not me."

"His fucking smug face." Anger returned to Franklin's voice. "I just want to kick his teeth in."

"Come on, Seth," Rosario said. He put her hand on the side of his neck. "Let's go to bed."

She was right. Bed was preferable to listening to the two men bicker. "Okay. Carry on, trusty steed." He laughed again, highly amused with himself, as she pushed.

As their voices trailed away, he heard one last comment. "It's time to send a message and remind everyone who's really in charge here."

But with sex and booze on his mind, Seth gave it no thought.

CHAPTER 49

Wyatt chucked a tattered tennis ball through the cool, dry air and watched as Supper bounded after it. He was amazed at how fast the three-legged dog could move. And even more amazed at how much he'd missed him.

He glanced to the side where Barbara sat on a bench and stared at nothing, a bottle of wine her only companion. In between repeated toss/fetch cycles, Wyatt moved closer and closer to her until he was near enough to be heard without speaking above a whisper.

"Remember how much you wanted to eat this dog?" He asked.

"Barbara blinked and looked at him. "What?"

"When I found him, and we thought he was going to die. All of you thought we should eat him."

She gave a slight smirk at that. "Supper," she said. "I wonder how he'd have tasted."

Supper stopped in place, looked at her, and gave a quick *Bark*.

Wyatt laughed. "I don't think he appreciates your curiosity."

"Probably not."

Wyatt extended the ball to her. "Want to give it a toss?"

Barb accepted and made a half-hearted throw. Supper looked at him, as if conveying *Lame* before trotting after it.

Wyatt took the opportunity to take a seat beside his mother, putting himself between her and the wine. He rested his hand on her knee.

"How are you holding up, mom?" He asked.

"I'm fine."

"I mean for real. No BS. Are you going to be okay?"

She looked at him, her eyes glistening with tears. "I'll muddle through."

Her words carried no weight and he realized she might be even further gone than he realized. "I can't even imagine how hard all of this has been on you."

"On me?" She asked. "You were shot. You almost died. Don't worry about me and take care of yourself."

"I want to take care of all of us. And to do that, we need to leave this place."

She gasped as if that were the most shocking thing she'd ever heard. "What? You were just..." She paused, considering the right word. "Promoted. Why do you want to leave now?"

Wyatt began to wonder if this plan had any chance. He'd figured his mother, who'd lost her only friend here, would be easiest to convince. "Because it's only a matter of time before they make me build a new army and lead another attack. How do you think that's going to go?"

She didn't answer.

"Mom, this is all a mirage. It looks good from a distance but when you get close enough you realize it's not at all what you were promised. This place is toxic."

She stayed silent for a long while. Supper returned with the ball three more times before she spoke again.

"Your brother will never leave."

"If he chooses Papa over us, then maybe he should stay behind."

Barbara flinched. He saw her clenched hands grinding in her lap. "I can't leave him, Wyatt. I can't keep losing people."

He understood. "If I can convince him, you'd go?"

His mother nodded. "Of course."

Supper dropped the ball into Wyatt's lap, but he didn't throw it that time. He was too busy trying to find a way for all of them to get out.

What he never saw was Franklin standing in the shadows of the casino, listening to every word he'd said.

CHAPTER 50

Wyatt cornered Seth before the day's festivities began. He'd waited for Rosario to leave the room, probably to fetch them breakfast, until he made his move.

He banged on the door and waited, bouncing on his feet, his body full of nerves. This had to work. He had to get through to his brother, otherwise everything he'd endured was for nothing.

After half a minute he heard Seth's wheels on the tile floor. "Forget your key, Rosie?" He opened the door, blinking sleep from his eyes as he found Wyatt instead of his girlfriend.

"Morning, brother," Seth said with a yawn.

Wyatt pushed into Seth's room and closed the door behind him.

"Yeah, sure, come on in," Seth said.

Wyatt didn't bother with pleasantries. "Seth, I'm not going to waste your time."

"Good man."

"Have you ever thought about getting out of here?" Wyatt asked.

Seth flashed his Cheshire cat grin. "Stop fucking with me."

"I'm serious."

Seth's eyes narrowed, his expression now wary. "*This* is what we left home for, Wyatt. This place. It's everything we wanted. I mean, fuck, Papa just named you the Protector. We're going to run this place, brother!"

This wasn't the way Wyatt had hoped the conversation would go but he'd known it was in the realm of possibilities. Maybe even expected it. "This ego trip shit? I don't want that. I don't want to be in charge of anything. I want to live a normal life, that's all."

"Normal," Seth huffed. "That's easy for you to say. You're not some one-legged asshole in a wheelchair." Seth rolled his chair into Wyatt's legs. "I'm never going to be normal, Wyatt. You think a woman like Rosario would give me a second look if it wasn't for my place here? The power I have?"

"Come on. You're letting Papa get inside your head. You'd don't need to be someone's lapdog to matter."

As soon as the words were out of his mouth, Wyatt knew that was a mistake. Seth's face went cold, his eyes blazed.

"You laugh at me, brother. You always have. You pretended to take care of me, but it was all about you. Wyatt, Wyatt, Wyatt being the good brother. Being the noble one." He pounded his remaining leg. "If I wasn't in this fucking chair, people would see me! But you know what? Papa appreciates me."

Seth took a deep breath, then another. Some of the anger left him. "When Yahweh takes Papa home, I'm going to take his place. And then everyone will see what I can do."

Wyatt still couldn't swallow what Seth was saying to him. "You really drank the Kool-Aid, little brother."

His lips pouted and he could feel his emotions spilling over. He was ready to cry at what had become of Seth. He didn't want to leave his brother behind, but if he stayed, he risked losing everything. And that he couldn't do. "I love you Seth, but I'm leaving. We all are."

Seth shook his head. "I love you, too Wyatt. But I can't let that happen." Seth nodded and Wyatt realized he was signaling to someone further back in the suite. He spun around but was too late. Glass shattered against his head and he crumpled to his knees.

When he looked up, he saw Franklin towering above him, the remnants of a vase in his hand. Then Seth wheeled around and came into view.

"Wyatt, I'm sorry. But maybe it would've been better for you if you had just stayed dead."

Franklin swung the thick, heavy bottom of the vase at Wyatt's face.

"This is for the greater good," Seth said.

And then everything disappeared.

CHAPTER 51

THE BEST WAY TO AVOID A HANGOVER WAS TO STAY DRUNK. THAT information had served Barbara well over the last couple months and it kept her head from spinning today too.

Despite a good buzz, the constant thudding of the music and the boisterous chatter of the partygoers made her want to retreat to her room with a bottle. She liked a good party as much as anyone, but this was a little much.

She scanned the crowd for Wyatt. She hadn't seen him all day and wondered if he'd had a chance to talk to Seth yet.

The idea of leaving scared her. The constant danger of life on the road was too fresh in her mind. But she knew her son was right. This place was sour. And she needed a new beginning.

As far as she could tell, Wyatt hadn't shown up for lunch, which had been an even better spread than the previous day's. Even though her belly was full of booze, she managed to down a plateful.

Seth sat at the front of the room, to Papa's right. Franklin sat on the left. Barbara had just begun to make her way toward him, to ask about Wyatt, when Papa grabbed the microphone.

"Does everyone have a full belly?" He asked.

The crowd answered in the affirmative.

"Good, good. Because this feast has been supplied to us by Yahweh himself. And what do we say to Yahweh?"

"Thank you!" The crowd roared.

"Exactly," Papa said. "Now that we have enjoyed His bounty, it is time for us to give back."

Papa stood, a movement that took considerable effort and time. His white, linen clothing did little to conceal his colossal girth, but it also gave him an undeniable presence as he addressed his followers.

"It has been many years since we've celebrated the tombola. Some of you have never witnessed the glory of this palaver, but today we remedy that!"

"We love you, Papa!" A woman shouted from the crowd. "We trust you!"

Papa shared a grandfatherly chuckle. "I thank you for that child. But it is not me who deserves the credit. It is in Yahweh that I trust."

More cheers.

Barbara rolled her eye. She had heard it all, day in and day out and she'd grown to loathe the constant God bothering. It would be one thing if Papa preached the bible or spoke about Christ, about love and forgiveness, but this was more the rambling of a TV evangelist whose ultimate goal was filling his personal coffer. Maybe these people believed Papa's schtick, but she did not.

"It is now time that we repay Yahweh for all that He has done for us."

Papa's guards stepped into view. Each held a large basket filled with folded pieces of paper. They brought them to the big man and set them at his feet. He nodded to them and they left.

"My children, the tombola has begun!"

CHAPTER 52

Sᴇᴛʜ ᴡᴀᴛᴄʜᴇᴅ ᴛʜᴇ ɢᴏɪɴɢs ᴏɴ, ʜɪs ʜᴇᴀʀᴛ ʀᴀᴄɪɴɢ. Hᴇ ᴋɴᴇᴡ this was a defining moment. That he was part of something bigger than him. Bigger than Papa. That he was going to see Yahweh's power at work.

He took no pleasure in what happened to his brother. It was necessary because Wyatt didn't understand. Wyatt didn't *believe*. If Wyatt was here, he would have caused a spectacle and shamed his family. Sometimes unpleasant things had to be done. That was the way of the world.

Seth reached over and took Rosario's hand. It was cool and damp. She pulled back.

"Everything's going to be alright," Seth whispered. "You just need to have faith."

Rosario wouldn't, couldn't, meet his gaze. She jumped up and scurried away, moving through the crowd and toward the casino. He couldn't understand why she was so scared. Nothing bad was going to happen to her, or to him. Papa wouldn't allow that. Sometimes he wondered if he'd ever understand women.

Seth watched her for a moment, but soon enough his attention was drawn back to Papa.

He motioned toward the baskets. "On these pieces of paper are your names," Papa said to the crowd. Every man and woman in the community. That includes Seth." Papa pointed at him. "Franklin." The tall man nodded to the crowd. "And myself, of course. Because I am not above any one of you. In Yahweh's eyes we are all equals. I am nothing but His vessel."

Papa plunged a hand into each bowl. "Are you ready for the drawing?" He asked.

"Yes!" the crowd roared.

Papa smiled. As he did Seth noticed thin, viscous fluid draining from the sores on his face. That intermixed in with the sweat which poured from his brow. Between the exertion of standing and the frenzy of the moment, he looked as if he'd just gone the distance in a marathon.

The big man rummaged through the baskets, digging, diving. He had a flair for the dramatic and dragged the moment out for just the right amount of time before stepping back.

In each hand he held a paper. And then he turned to Seth.

"Seth, I want you to close your eyes and pray. Ask Yahweh to take control of your voice, your mouth, and tell me what He says."

Seth did as told even though he wasn't entirely sure what he was supposed to do. So, he asked God for guidance. Asked him to give him the answer Papa sought. There was nothing but silence at first, so he squeezed his eyes tighter and asked again.

Please, God, tell me what I'm supposed to say.

And then he knew.

He opened his eyes and looked to the crowd. Then he turned to Papa.

"Left hand." Seth said.

Papa gave a slow nod. He dropped the paper he'd held in his right hand. It fluttered to the floor and landed by Seth's feet.

Then, Papa opened his left hand. He opened the piece of paper, silently read what was written on it, and beamed. "Yahweh has made His decision."

CHAPTER 53

Wyatt had regained consciousness a few hours earlier, coming to in a locked hotel room on the third floor. A room that gave him a bird's eye view of the celebration going on thirty-odd feet below.

His head still rung like a bell and he was weary of the ongoing, nonstop noise of the party. It was only when that noise stopped that he decided to pay attention again.

Through the glass he saw Papa, flanked by Seth and Franklin, stand. It made Wyatt sick to look at them, especially Seth. He was still reeling after his brother's betrayal and vowed that, if he ever saw him again, he'd punch him in the mouth.

But he doubted he'd get that chance. They had him locked in this room, far away from everyone else, for a reason and he suspected that reason was to kill him.

He remembered the day, months earlier, that he'd thought about taking Supper and leaving the casino. Why hadn't he listened to his gut?

But playing the what if game would serve no good. He needed to focus on the now and try to figure a way out of this mess.

He'd already tried breaking the lock on the door. Tried smashing the glass. Neither worked. His only chance was waiting and hoping an opportunity arose.

Wyatt watched Papa's new guards set two baskets by his feet. From the distance it looked like they were filled with cotton or fabric. Then he saw the fat man reach into each one.

After Papa removed his hands, Wyatt heard his voice over the speakers. He heard him ask Seth to pray for an answer and he heard Seth supply one.

Despite his pessimism, he was in no way ready for what came next.

CHAPTER 54

Seth thought he'd heard wrong. This wasn't possible. This couldn't be Yahweh's plan. This was wrong.

Then he saw her moving toward the front of the crowd. He hadn't heard wrong at all. But that realization only made things worse.

She smiled nervously as she stepped forward. Seth knew she didn't like being the center of attention and that this must be awkward and overwhelming for her. But she pushed past it because she was strong, even if she didn't believe she was.

This can't be happening, Seth thought. It's some horrible error.

Seth wheeled up to Papa and pulled at his shirt, not even considering how inappropriate it was.

"Please, Papa, no. You can't do this." Seth had the sense to keep his voice low so the microphone wouldn't catch it.

Papa leaned down and Seth could smell the rot drifting from his face. His eyes were red and wild. "Son, I'm not doing anything. I made no choice. You did. Yahweh did. I just read what was on the paper." Papa turned back to the crowd.

But Seth wasn't done. He clawed at Papa's meaty arm. "No, I

made a mistake. I meant to say right hand. Right hand! You have to switch it!"

Papa turned to Seth, grinning in a way that bared his teeth. "I love you Seth, like my own son. But the announcement has been made. This is Yahweh's will. And if you push this issue any further, this isn't going to end well for you either. You understand?"

Seth opened his mouth but saw the look in Papa's eyes. He slumped back into his chair and wheeled away. As he did the dropped paper got caught in his footrest, but he paid it no attention. If he could have fled, he would have, but Seth knew that would only exacerbate the situation. So, he stayed and watched as Franklin reached out and took her hand.

Franklin gave her a brief embrace, then turned her to face the madding crowd. As they roared, Seth began to cry silent tears.

"My children," Papa said. "Give up your thanks to Allie Hagan!"

CHAPTER 55

WYATT KNEW THIS WAS GOING TO BE TERRIBLE, BUT HE FORCED himself to watch. He'd promised her he'd keep her safe and failed so this was his penance. He'd have to live the remainder of his days, no matter how few or plenty, with the guilt.

He'd failed her.

Papa's voice boomed through the speakers. "My dearest Allie, I cannot thank you enough for this. I know you are new to our ways so this must all be something of a shock to you."

Wyatt could see her nervous smile. She still hadn't realized what was coming. He didn't know the specifics, but he was certain of the outcome and he was helpless to stop it.

As Franklin retrieved a large, metal basin and set in at Allie's feet, Wyatt slammed his fists against the unbreakable windows. He screamed and shouted. He swore and cried. He knew it was pointless, that no one could hear him and, even if they could, they wouldn't raise so much as a finger to help.

Her fate was sealed.

And it was his fault.

"My beautiful child, Yahweh Himself has chosen you. Do you realize how special you are?"

Allie gave a tense titter. "Not really."

"Well, let me assure you, you are very, very special." Papa patted her shoulder. "Now, please kneel."

That's when she caught on. Wyatt saw her eyes widen; nerves replaced with fear. Her body tensed and she went to move but Franklin grabbed her by the shoulders and held her in place.

His mouth moved and even at the distance Wyatt could read his lips. "Kneel, bitch."

Allie refused, so Franklin pushed her to her knees. She hit the ground hard and Wyatt knew she was crying, maybe in pain but more likely in terror.

And it was his fault.

"My children, never forget this day, for on this day you are witnessing both the glory and the vengeance of Yahweh! Because though he is a kind and merciful presence in our lives, he also demands sacrifice!"

Wyatt could feel the room reverberating from the frenzy of the crowd. They were like wild animals, but worse because they should know better. They should have mercy. But they had none.

Allie struggled to free herself, but Franklin held tight. He had her by eight inches and sixty pounds. She had no chance.

Papa pulled a blade, the same blade he'd use to disembowel Vern, from under the table. "Yahweh demands to be fed and today we acquiesce to his needs! Praise, Yahweh!"

The crowd shouted, "Praise Yahweh!"

"Praise Yahweh!" Papa repeated.

"Praise Yahweh!" The crowd bellowed.

"Let this blood both wash away our sins and satiate his needs!" He looked down at Allie. "Thank you for your service, my child."

Wyatt fought every urge to squeeze his eyes closed and forced himself to watch as Papa slit her throat from ear to ear. Her body spasmed and flailed as the life gushed from her and into the bucket.

Then Franklin yanked her head back, turning the gash into a gaping wound. Blood rushed out of her like water over Niagara Falls. Her entire body spasmed. And then she went limp.

When she stopped bleeding, Franklin dropped her body to the side of the container. Papa reached into the bucket, soaking his hand in Allie's hot blood.

He then retracted it and turned to Franklin. The man bent at the waist and Papa painted a series of lines and circles across his cheeks and brown. When he was finished, Franklin smiled, pleased.

Then Papa looked back to his people.

"Praise Yahweh!" He said one more time. "And come to me."

As the community lined up to receive their blessing, Wyatt allowed himself to look away. He dropped to his knees, sobbing. Allie was dead.

And it was his fault.

CHAPTER 56

Day had shifted to dusk when Wyatt heard the keys jingle on the other side of the door. They were coming for him now. To kill him, probably. And that might be better for everyone.

He steeled himself, ready for whoever it was to come in and finish him off, only to have Rosario dash into the room as the door opened. Her make-up ran down her face in black rivulets and her eyes were swollen from crying.

"I'm so sorry, Wyatt." She swallowed hard, staring at the broken man in front of her.

Wyatt climbed to his feet. "Did Seth know?"

Rosario shook her head. "We knew about the sacrifice. But had no idea it would be Allie."

"You're sure about that?"

She nodded, sending her hair flying around her face. And he believed her.

"I want to get away from this place," she said. "I want to go with you, and your mother. If you'll have me."

He barely knew this woman, but he could see in her eyes that she wanted out as bad as he did. "Alright."

She stared, wary. "You'll take me?"

Wyatt nodded. "Yes. Now go get my mother and take her to the rear gate. Hide somewhere until I get there. And give me those keys."

She still held them in her fist and handed them over. He knew they were the master set, the same kind he'd found on Doctor Ramona after she was killed. And they'd do just fine.

"Come with me," Rosario said. "Let's go now."

Wyatt shook his head. "I'll be there in an hour. But there's something I have to do first."

He started toward the door, but Rosario blocked him. "Don't Wyatt. Seth's a lost cause. And they'll kill you if they see you."

Wyatt stiff-armed his way past her. "You're in charge of my mother. I'll handle everything else."

CHAPTER 57

WYATT USED THE SERVICE WORKERS' CORRIDORS AND MADE IT
to the armory without being noticed. From the sounds, the party was
dying down outside, and he heard people shuffling indoors. He had
to be quick and careful.

As he entered the room, he saw Alexander's locker and almost
lost it. What would Alexander have thought about what happened
here today? What would he think about him? There was no time for
that now.

He pulled the keys from his pocket and unlocked several of the
cabinets. He grabbed a duffel bag and filled it with pistols and magazines. Then he chambered a round in one and tucked it into his belt.

He wished he could take the AKs, but they were too bulky and
he needed to be discreet. Nonetheless, the vision of charging outside
and mowing everyone down Tony Montana style was almost too
good to pass up. Going out in a blaze of glory didn't sound bad at all
right about now.

But he had more important things to do, including keeping his
mother alive. He zipped the bag closed and almost left the room

when he saw an Army green hard case that he'd missed in his earlier visit to this room.

Wyatt knew cases like this usually housed valuable firearms and his curiosity got the best of him. He knelt, popped the lid, and found something even better than guns.

The case was full of explosives and he knew exactly how he could use them.

Assuming every other aspect of his plan went perfect.

WYATT JOGGED DOWN THE HALLWAY, TOWARD FRANKLIN'S room. He had no idea if the man was inside but didn't care. If he wasn't, then Wyatt would wait until he showed up and blow his brains out the second, he stepped through the door. He wanted - needed - to kill that motherfucker before he left otherwise this was all for nothing.

As he passed by Papa's room, he heard movement and voices. He heard fucking. The fat bastard must be having a celebratory orgy in there.

Wyatt almost changed course and stormed into Papa's suite, but he knew that would be a mistake. Papa might be a snake, but Franklin was the one who made it personal. Wyatt was certain of that.

When he came to Franklin's door, he grabbed the keys, then paused. He could hear crying. And he knew who it was.

Seth's door hung ajar and Wyatt didn't pause as he pushed it open and stepped inside. His brother sat in the main quarters; his back turned to him. His upper body shook with sobs.

What did the little fuck have to cry about? He didn't have to watch his girlfriend get slaughtered.

"The greater good, right?" Wyatt said. His voice was barely a whisper.

Seth was startled and craned his neck to look around. His eyes were bloodshot and swollen. "Wyatt, I'm so sorry," he said.

Wyatt didn't hear him. When he saw the rust-colored dried blood - Allie's blood - painted on Seth's face all he could vengeance.

He rushed at him and grabbed Seth by the throat. He squeezed, his knuckles flaring white. His nails digging into his skin. His entire body shook as he choked the life out of his brother.

Seth grabbed at his hands, trying to pry them off. But Wyatt wasn't going to let that happen. He squeezed harder.

"Allie's dead because of you! And I couldn't do anything about it because you set me up! Did you know that fucking Franklin locked me in a room so I could watch it happen? Did you?"

He was spitting his words on his brother's face. He felt the rage course through him.

"It... wasn't..." Seth began. Wyatt continued to squeeze. He didn't want to hear anything his brother had to say.

Seth shook his head and cried harder.

Wyatt watched his brother choke. The brother he'd protected for so long. The brother he'd loved.

Seth's eyes looked ready to bulge from their sockets. Snot ran from his nose. Drool from his mouth. He'd be dead soon.

Wyatt released, stumbling backward. Seth dragged in a ragged breath, coughing as he grabbed at his throat.

"I didn't know," he said after he made a partial recovery. "I believed it was up to God until I saw this."

Seth reached into his pocket. Wyatt was so distrusting that he almost expected his brother to pull out a gun, or maybe a ninja star, something to kill him with. Instead, he held a piece of paper.

"What is that?" Wyatt asked.

"The other paper Papa pulled from the basket. The one in his right hand."

Wyatt snatched it away from him and examined it. There was nothing on the front. Nothing on the back.

"It's blank," he said.

Seth nodded. "I know. They all were." His voice cracked in a sob. "It was all a lie," he said. "There was no choice. No divine intervention. Papa lied to me."

His voice dissolved into more crying and whatever anger Wyatt clung to faded away. But he still couldn't forgive him.

"We're leaving. Rosario's coming too." Wyatt heard Seth gasp as he moved to the door. "I'll miss the person you used to be."

"Wyatt. I'm sorry about everything," Seth said.

"So am I, brother." Wyatt said, leaving Seth alone in the dark.

CHAPTER 58

Seth sat outside Papa's room as Keith, one of the new guards, opened the door.

"I need to see Papa," Seth said.

Keith glanced into the suite. Seth looked past him and saw the door to Papa's bedroom was closed.

"He's indisposed at the moment," Keith said when he turned back to Seth.

"I'm sure he is, but I have information he needs to know right now. Information that cannot wait."

Keith sighed and Seth knew he'd got his way, as usual. "Alright. But tell him you demanded access. I don't want him bitching me out."

"Don't worry. When he hears what I have to tell him you'll be the last thing on his mind."

As Seth wheeled himself into the room his mind raced. He couldn't believe his brother and mother were abandoning him, that they had turned their backs on him. He understood Wyatt's anger, but they were family. That was supposed to be more important than anything. And Rosario too. In one fell swoop he'd lost almost everyone he loved.

And now it was time for revenge.

As he neared Papa's bedroom, Owen, the other guard, rapped on Papa's door.

"Papa, Seth's here to see you. We tried to send him away, but he insisted."

"It'sssss fiiiii..." Papa's slurred words seeped through and Owen gave the knob a turn.

Seth pushed it the rest of the way open and found Papa's gargantuan body sprawled across the bed. His frame nearly filled the queen-sized mattress, leaving just scraps of space for two of his wives who laid nude beside him. Papa himself was clad only in a pair of boxer shots. At least he was wearing something, Seth thought as he entered the room.

He shut the door behind him, and continued to Papa who watched him with drunken, bleary eyes.

"I need your counsel, Papa," Seth said. "And to tell something only meant for your ears."

Papa swiveled his head toward his wives, who existed somewhere between sleep and unconsciousness. "They're not to be concerned with. Come to me, my son."

Seth aligned his chair beside the bed. Papa's body threw off heat like a boiler and Seth saw the bed around him was saturated with so much sweat that it was pooling in low spots.

Papa reached out and dropped his moist hand over Seth's thigh. He smiled, the loving, benevolent expression Seth knew so well. This man was his mentor. His hero. The person he aspired to become.

"Everyone's leaving me. My mother, Wyatt, Rosario. They're heading out now unless someone stops them."

"Are they now?" Papa asked.

Seth nodded. "They're leaving because of the tombola. Because Allie was the sacrifice."

Papa gave a melancholy nod, his bottom lip bulging in a pout. "Sad. Very sad. But we cannot question Yahweh's wishes."

"I know."

"They don't understand." Papa waved his hand, beckoning Seth closer. "Weak people with small minds try to drag everyone great down to their level." He drew in a hitching breath. "And my boy, my son, Seth, the next in line." Papa's voice fell back into a drunken garble. "You aaaaaare meant fer... great thingssss."

Seth sniffled, fighting back tears. "I know, Papa."

Papa rolled onto his side, an act that stole even more of his breath. "You're the future for this community. I know that you are meant for thissss."

Seth leaned in and put his right arm around the big man, embracing him. He didn't care that he was almost naked, or that he was a clammy, disgusting mess. None of it mattered because he worshipped him.

"Thank you for believing in me when nobody else would. When everybody else just saw me as an anchor in this shitty excuse for the world. As someone that could never survive let alone thrive."

Papa placed his hand on the back of Seth's head, stroking his hair haphazardly. "Of course, son. It's because I love you so much."

Seth gave up on holding back the tears. They came freely, raining onto Papa's skin. "Before I came to see you, I prayed for a very long time."

Papa nodded. "That's good. In times of strife we must turn to Yahweh for answers."

Seth wiped at his weeping eyes. "And He did. He answered me." He stared into Papa's eyes, trying to remember the last time he loved someone this much.

"Papa, I have a message for you from God," Seth's words came out in a whisper.

Papa leaned in closer. Their faces were millimeters apart. "Tell me."

With his left hand Seth reached into the gap between his leg and the chair. He pulled out the butcher's knife he'd brought from his room, and sunk it into Papa's belly.

The blade plunged into the flesh and Seth yanked the knife toward him as he stabbed. His hand sunk deep into the wound and he felt Papa's fat envelop his fist, but he refused to stop.

Seth jerked the knife from one side of Papa's stomach to the next, then watched as his guts tumbled free. They rolled off the bed and splashed onto the floor. Gallons of intestines and blood and organs.

Through it all Papa never said a word. And he never broke eye contact with Seth.

Only when Seth pulled the knife free and dropped it into the steaming pile of innards, did Papa's head fall back onto the bed. He gave three brief, gasping wheezes. And died.

Seth looked to the wives who were still enjoying their alcohol-fueled slumber and hadn't heard a thing. Then he turned his chair and wheeled himself to the bedroom door.

When he opened it, he saw the guards sitting at the kitchen table playing a game of cards. He made certain to hide his gory left hand as they glanced his way.

"Papa's in the bathroom and would like some privacy. I don't think today's feast is sitting well," Seth said.

Keith wrinkled his nose. "Must've been those damn enchiladas."

They returned their attention to the game of seven card stud and didn't give him so much as another look as he rolled out of the room.

CHAPTER 59

Sᴍ Sɪʀᴇɴs ʙʟᴀʀᴇᴅ ᴀs Wʏᴀᴛᴛ ʟᴏᴀᴅᴇᴅ ᴛʜᴇ ᴡᴇᴀᴘᴏɴs ᴀɴᴅ sᴜᴘᴘʟɪᴇs he'd stolen into, of all things, a shopping cart.

"Hurry, Wyatt!" Rosario said in a voice between a whisper and a shout, if such a thing was possible.

He could hear voices and he knew they were heading their way. He turned to his mother who handed him case after case of canned goods for him to deposit into the cart. "This is like old times, huh mom?"

Barbara nodded and, to his surprise, smiled. She looked more alive, more alert, than she had since he'd returned to the casino. Maybe this was what she needed, to get away from this awful place, in order to find herself again. He could hope, anyway.

Just a few cases to go. Almost there.

Supper barked, frenzied and excited. The bark he used when he saw someone. Shit, Wyatt thought, we only needed a few more minutes.

"Trying to run off without me?" A voice asked.

Wyatt recognized it, but he had to be wrong. His ears were playing tricks on him.

He turned and saw Seth racing their way, as fast as his arms could push. "I know I told you to feel free to leave me behind if shit got real, but I didn't think you'd actually do it," Seth said.

Wyatt didn't know what to think. His brother sounded more like the Seth he'd grown up with and loved than the disciple he'd become the past few months. But could he trust him?

"This because of you?" Wyatt pointed to one of the overhead sirens which wailed incessantly.

"Yeah, but probably not how you're thinking."

"I'm thinking you ratted us out."

"Shit, brother. I'm a lot of things but I ain't no snitch."

Seth held up the knife and his bloody hand. "I killed Papa."

Wyatt again couldn't believe that he'd hear, but Seth's arm was soaked with blood from his fingers to his elbow. And it clearly wasn't his blood.

He wanted to say something but, before he could, Rosario ran to Seth and threw her arms around him. "I'm sorry. I didn't think you would ever--"

"I'm the one that's sorry. They got inside my head," Seth said.

Rosario kissed him and Wyatt smiled. Finally, something good was happening after these months of hell.

And then came the gunshot.

Rosario fell into Seth, collapsing against him. She slithered down his body in slow motion before dropping to the pavement.

Seth stared at her, panicked and confused. Wyatt peeled his eyes off his brother and Rosario and looked past them.

And saw Franklin.

A leering grin was plastered to his face. "Damn, you Morrill's are unlucky in love." He pointed the pistol at Wyatt. "What is that o for three?"

"You motherfucker!" Seth screamed. He went to spin his chair around but only made it halfway before Franklin trained the gun on him.

"Ah, ah, ah. Don't try it, boy. I'm a good shot. If you don't believe me, ask your girlfriend." He laughed. "She might be slow to answer though."

Wyatt watched, trying to decide when to make his move, but someone else made his decision moot.

Supper soared through the air, jaws chomping down on Franklin's wrist. As the dog's teeth ripped at his flesh the man dropped the gun which skittered across the concrete.

With Franklin trying to fight off the dog, Wyatt grabbed a pistol from the shopping cart and chambered a round. He aimed, but the tussle between Franklin and his dog was too crazed to take a shot.

"Supper! Come!"

Immediately the dog let go. Franklin kicked, botting the dog in the back end and eliciting a pained yelp.

That was the final straw.

With Supper out of the way, Wyatt shot. The bullet caught Franklin in the side, and he spun around before dropping to a knee. Wyatt shot again, but that one missed.

Shouting voices, dozens of them, rushed toward his group and stole his attention. He looked and saw what seemed to be every asshole in the casino rushing their way.

They had to get out of here and fast, but first he wanted to end the son of a bitch who'd killed his girlfriend and kicked his dog.

But when he looked back to Franklin, the man was gone.

"We have to go, Wyatt!" Barbara screamed.

She was right.

"Take the cart," Wyatt said.

As she did, Wyatt grabbed the handles of Seth's wheelchair. His little brother was sobbing as he clutched Rosario's lifeless hand between his own.

"I'm sorry, brother, but we'll have to mourn later."

He didn't wait for Seth to answer. He ran.

CHAPTER 60

They made it to the border, which thankfully was only a few hundred yards from the casino. It was about time something worked out in their favor.

Scores of rusted out cars sat against the large wall, which looked identical to the one that had stopped them months earlier. There was no point of entry, but Wyatt had planned for that.

"So, what now," Seth asked.

Barbara pulled out the green hard case and opened the lid to reveal the explosives.

"Now, we make a door," she said.

She quickly dug a small indentation in the dirt next to the wall, tucked the bomb into it, then packed dirt around to hold it in place.

"How do you know what you're doing?" Seth asked.

"I read the instructions," she said, some of the old moxie returning to her voice.

And Wyatt loved hearing it. As she finished, he scanned the desert and saw pinpricks of light in the distance behind them. They'd lost their pursuers in the darkness, but the mob hadn't given up.

"Get behind the cars," Barbara said.

Supper jumped in Seth's lap and Wyatt took them a good distance away from where the explosives were planted. The four of them hunkered behind a dilapidated VW van and Barbara raised the detonator.

"You ready?" she asked.

"I'm not--" Seth didn't get to finish his sentence.

Barbara pushed the button and the bomb went off in an instant. Chunks of dirt fell from the sky and dust shrouded everything around them.

If the mob wasn't sure where to find them before, they sure as hell would now.

"We need to go," Wyatt led the way.

They dashed to the wall where a hole at least ten feet across had been blasted through. He stepped through, for some reason expecting things to be different in Mexico, but it was just more desert. More nothing.

It was too dark to see very far south. Only a black void. One Wyatt was ready to jump into.

That's when the gunfire kicked off.

The mob had caught up to them.

Damn, that was fast, Wyatt thought.

They took cover behind the southern side of the wall as bullets plinked against the metal. They were safe behind the steel, Wyatt knew, at least for a few moments. Until the others came through the hole they'd just made.

Barbara dug through the shopping cart and pulled out guns. She passed one to each of her sons.

"What's the plan?" Seth asked. "Do we wait for them to join us south of the border or start shooting back all willy nilly?"

"I vote to wait," Wyatt said.

"I vote for willy nilly," Barbara said.

"I guess that makes me the tiebreaker." Seth raised an eyebrow.

Wyatt smiled at him. "Well? Which is it?"

"I say we--"

High, feral shouts cut off his words. Wyatt knew the sound immediately - cannibals.

They must have heard the sirens blaring and took that signal for weakness, for a chance to attack. Good planning, Wyatt thought.

Screams and yelps and cries of pain volleyed over the wall.

There was a smattering of return fire but not much. Wyatt knew the mob had little in the way of firearms because he'd stolen almost all the pistols and hidden the ammunition for the rifles.

With no way of fighting back, all the community from the casino could do was run. And they ran toward the wall. It sounded like a stampede of horses coming their way and Wyatt knew nothing good awaited.

"We have to run!" He shouted to his family. And they did.

Behind them was a chorus of battle. Cannibals whooping and yelling, people dying, guns firing. And pain. So much pain.

As they ran Wyatt glanced back and saw a handful of shapes of humans pass through the hole. Some of them were firing backward, at whoever was shooting at them, but most shot ahead. At them.

"Up there!" One of them said. "Those fuckers that killed Papa are getting away!"

Wyatt heard bullets zip through the air. Saw them kick up dirt. Felt the cool breeze as they soared by, too close.

He fired blindly behind him, not expecting to hit anyone, but hoping to slow them down or force them to hit the ground. It didn't seem to be working.

They continued to flee but bullets kept coming at them. He spotted a boulder ahead, one big enough to provide cover for all of them. "Up there!"

Wyatt got Seth behind the rock and his brother dove from his chair and to the ground. He held Supper beside him to keep the dog safe.

Bullets pinged off the rock, blowing out chunks as they ricocheted wildly.

Wyatt peered around the edge, aimed, shot.

A man fell to the ground with a grunt. Wyatt aimed to shoot again, but incoming fire sent him diving to the ground.

He landed beside his mother and reached out, grabbing her arm. "Get behind the rock," he said, wondering what she was waiting for.

She didn't answer. He looked at her, but it was so dark it took him a minute to see her hands holding her neck.

And to see the blood gushing through her fingers.

"Mom!"

In the midst of the melee she'd been shot, and he hadn't even realized. What kind of son lets that happen?

Barbara's eyes were wide and glassy. Blood drained from her mouth.

"Seth! Oh fuck, Seth!" Wyatt screamed as he watched his mother bleed, helpless.

It wasn't like Seth could make this better, but he couldn't think of anything else to say, anything else to do.

"Seth!" He repeated. Panic threatened to take over, but he couldn't let that happen. He had to stay calm and keep his mother alive.

"Wyatt?" Seth said. His voice was anything but calm.

Wyatt turned to his brother who frantically and silently pointed south like the world's worst mime. He followed his gesticulations and saw what had his little brother so scared.

There were hundreds of them, stretching as far into the dark as they could see.

Rows of sticks planted in the ground. But they weren't just sticks.

They were pikes. And on each one of them was topped with a rotting human head.

Behind the pike's, Wyatt saw figures emerging from the darkness. Coming toward them.

He heard his mother gurgle and returned his attention to her. Her eyes were no longer startled and glassy, they were dull. And closing.

"No, mom! Please hang on!" Wyatt screamed.

He tore off his shirt and pressed it against her neck but the river of blood that had flowed so free was already down to a trickle.

She was dying in his arms.

"Seth, I need your help!"

He glanced back at his brother who had both arms wrapped around Supper as the dog growled and snarled at the shadows approaching from the south. Wyatt had never seen his dog act so vicious and he wondered what type of evil the mutt sensed coming their way.

And he wondered, what fresh hell did we step into now?

THE END

AFTERWORD

We hope you enjoyed "Flesh of the Sons" which is book 2 in the "Cannibal Country" series. Book 3 will be available in 2020. And if you thought books 1 and 2 were crazy, buckle up, buttercup!

Please take a moment to sign up for our mailing lists where you'll get free stories and novellas and stay on top of all future releases.

Tony Urban's list - http://tonyurbanauthor.com/signup

Drew Strickland's list - https://www. subscribepage.com/u2x7bo_copy_copy

Printed in Great Britain
by Amazon